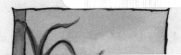

'Johnson's writing is witty and inventive, and the character of Thora ... is full of unexpectedness ... This is a book full of fun.' *Sunday Times* children's book of the week

'Thora is an irresistible character with an attitude that's all her own! Though modern in its telling, this tale has a timeless feel to it – storytelling at its best.' Starred review, *Publishing News*

'An attractively illustrated and uplifting story.' *Times Educational Supplement*

Look out for *Thora*, the first book about
everyone's favourite half-mermaid!

# Thora

## and the Green Sea-Unicorn

written and illustrated by
## Gillian Johnson

Hodder
Children's
Books

a division of Hodder Headline Limited

FOR Nicholas

110 %

Here is what I see
from the deck of our boat

River Thames

Houseboats galore

It's no sea·side town. This is a
BIG CITY HARBOUR and very noisy

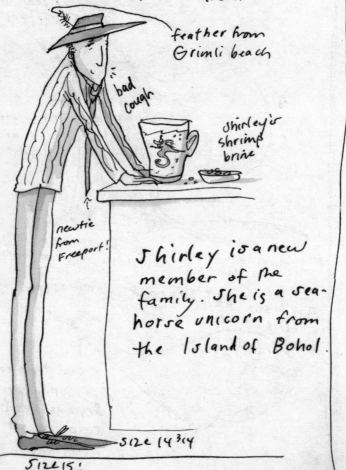

This tall man is Mr Walters, my Guardian Angle. He says he can already taste London in the back of his throat.

feather from Grimli beach

bad cough

Shirley's shrimp brine

newtie from Freeport!

Shirley is a new member of the family. She is a sea-horse unicorn from the Island of Bohol.

SIZE 14 ¾

SIZE 15!

Mr. Walters says that Shirley is as rare as a Bunyip in a Billabong.
(very very rare)
When she swims, she leaves a trail of sparkly lights.
Shirley
Shirley can write her name with her silver horn.

# chapter 1

If you had never met Thora, Halla and Mr Walters, and you saw them from the penthouse suite of the Saltworks Luxury Flats as they sailed up to Chelsea Wharf on a sunny day in late May, you might mistake them for an eccentric family out for a cruise on the Thames. But if you were Pamela P. Poutine, petty thief, smuggler of precious sea creatures and former B-grade film star, you'd know otherwise.

Here's what Pamela took in through a pair of sparkly pink opera glasses.

First, the peacock. Bright Bass Strait blue. Perched on the roof of the little houseboat cabin like a weather vane. No commercial value.

Next, the old geezer steering the boat. Very tall, thin as a string and dressed head to toe in cricket whites. Everything about him – face, nose, shoulders, legs – seemed long and narrow and white, as if he had been bleached and vertically stretched. His bamboo walking stick and trilby hat gave him the air of a viceroy. Yet he looked as if he'd blow over in a breeze. The grandfather?

A girl was passing him a box of tissues to blow his nose.

She was ten or eleven years old and dressed in a black one-piece body suit like the ones worn by surfers on the Cornish coast. Wetsuit? She looked a very odd figure – brown hair spraying like a fountain from where it was tied at the top of her head, a naughty smiling face, wide-spaced gimlet eyes. And what was that gleaming ring on a chain around her neck? It might be gold, but it was hard to tell. The girl was in constant motion, running, dancing around and chattering to the blonde who was swimming alongside the boat.

Yes, the blonde. Pamela adjusted her glasses. There was something fishy about the blonde.

People just didn't swim in the Thames on a May morning. It was cold even by Pamela's standards, and her own tail was rather well insulated. The blonde looked extremely at home in the icy water, suspiciously so, as if it *were* her home.

Either she was an unusually good swimmer, or …

Pamela peered hard.

Could it be?

The flash of purple iridescence confirmed it. The blonde was a mermaid – the first Pamela had seen since her departure from the sea floor all those years ago. The glimpse of the mermaid's tail filled Pamela with a sudden nostalgia, that sad, damp feeling that you get when you listen to a favourite old song. Then she noticed something in the mermaid's hand.

Something small and green. Very, *very* green.

With trembling hands Pamela adjusted the opera glasses. Her tail broke out in a shimmer, bright and (she noted) beautiful to behold. A smile tickled the edges of her mouth.

Yes, she was owed a little good luck.

She reached for the phone and dialled Mr Oto's direct line in Tokyo. She would not mention the mermaid. Mr Oto had long ago finished with mermaids. But a sea-unicorn was another matter.

# Chapter 2

'I think this calls for some Russian Caravan,' announced Mr Walters, glancing at one of the four old-fashioned watches that he wore on his bony wrist.

He could have passed for Thora's grandfather, but was actually her Guardian Angle. Like many people, Mr Walters liked to celebrate most events in life with a nice cup of tea. As he got older, the events worth celebrating grew smaller – a sportsman-like smile from a good fast bowler, the sighting of a giant marine turtle, a brand new pot of Gentleman's Relish. But this was a really, really big event: the family's arrival in London, Mr Walters' home town. It called for a whole pot out there on the deck of the *Loki*.

'You sit down,' Halla told him. 'We'll make the tea.'

Halla was Thora's mother and a mermaid, with clear glowing skin and long blonde hair that smelled faintly of pumpkin pie. She arranged the teacups on a tray while Thora poured the boiling water into the teapot.

Cosmo, Thora's pet peacock, stood close to Mr Walters and fanned his beautiful blue and green tail in the breeze.

'Stop showing off, Cosmo,' said Thora. She reached for the biscuit tin and threw some Monte Carlo biscuit crumbs in the bird's direction.

Thora was glad to be back on land. She missed her friends in Grimli – Holly, Ricky and Lynne. But on the long sea voyage that had followed her family's rather hasty departure, she'd gained an extremely unusual new friend.

Shirley was a stunning little sea-unicorn, half the length of a baby's arm and twice as strong. She had a mane of sparkling coral threads, a flexible, curly tail and a tubby little sea-horse belly. Using her wings and tail for propulsion, and her silver horn and long tubular snout to steer, Shirley moved through the water with the ease and grace of an aquatic flying machine.

Now, unicorns are rare enough. But a sea-unicorn is harder to find than a bunyip in a billabong. And each has its unique features. In Shirley's case, there were three things that set her apart from all other living creatures.

5

First, her colour. Green, but not the green of billiard tables or golf turf or emeralds or even jade. No, Shirley was the green of the most concentrated short-season moss found on far-flung lava fields in Iceland, brilliant and bejewelled as if with diamonds of morning dew.

Second, she left a sparkly silver trail behind her when she swam, a sort of scattering of tiny pinpoints of light that changed colour according to her mood.

And finally, her horn. It was a slightly knobbly appendage with a surprisingly sharp tip.

Shirley's origins were unclear. The nuns at the Filipino sea-horse orphanage (which was really a rather beautiful mangrove forest on the island of Bohol) had told her that her parents had abandoned her when she was a baby because her silver horn

frightened them. (In some Asian legends, a unicorn's horn is poisonous.) Shirley did not fit in at the orphanage, either. The other sea-horse orphans teased and bullied her, calling her a mutant and a freak. At the age of two, she had galloped away to see the world, hoping to find a place where she truly belonged.

With Mr Walters' and Halla's help, Thora had rescued Shirley

6

from a whirlpool in the South China Sea and she'd been with them ever since. For her size, Shirley was very strong and she could pull Thora along at a rate of five knots per hour. At night, she slept beside Thora's bed in a large glass jug carpeted with seaweed. She was stubborn, with a fierce temper that made her armour rattle. Though a little spoiled, her pocket size made everyone feel protective towards her. Mr Walters was particularly fond of Shirley and called her 'the Little Empress'.

Cosmo could be jealous at times, but he bore it stoically.

When they had finished their tea, Thora carried the tray to the kitchen sink to rinse the cups. Mr Walters wasn't eating much at the moment, but Thora was surprised to see that he had not even finished his tea.

This was very unusual.

Perhaps it had been too weak? The leaves *did* look a little old and shrivelled, like the tobacco leaves she had seen in mud puddles in Tobago. She made a mental note to replenish their supply of Russian Caravan.

# chapter 3

Though pleased to be back in London, Mr Walters was subdued. It had been a long, hard journey from Grimli-By-The-Sea.

The fever he'd been battling since leaping into the South China Sea to save Shirley was still with him. It was a shivery sort of flu that had settled into his long bones and made his hands tremble like the *Loki*'s TV antenna in a sea breeze. Halla was very worried about him and had insisted the *Loki* sail immediately for England, where he could receive some proper medical attention. But now everyone was fussing around him so much that he couldn't think straight. It was good to retire to his room for some peace and quiet.

Mr Walters had looked forward to returning to London – not because he wanted to see a doctor (Mr Walters disliked going to the doctor), but because London was his home. There were many old haunts that he wanted to visit and people he wanted to look up. But the person he wanted to see most of all was his old friend, Lionel Bidet. He felt impatient to get out of London and into the countryside, to Snug House where the Bidets lived in ramshackle splendour.

He closed the curtains and lay back on his lumpy bed with its slightly yellowed blue and white striped mattress that smelled of the sea. Oh, how he wished Mrs Walters were alive! What fun they would have had returning to Snugshire together. They had not been blessed with children but Mrs Walters had loved their godson, Jerome, like her own child. Jerome was the sole Bidet heir. Back then he'd been a funny little boy with gappy teeth and a cry like a wolverine. But he was all grown up now, with a daughter of his own.

Mr Walters' dearly departed Imogen had been famous for her perfect pot of tea. She always measured the leaves out with the cap of an old Pimm's bottle, and she never overbrewed. She was very opposed to tea bags when they became fashionable and forbade them in the house. He could just picture her warming the teapot then curling up like a cat in the chair by his bed.

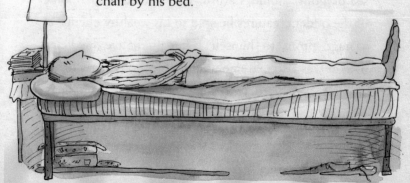

# chapter 4

'It's an extraordinary creature,' reported Pamela P. Poutine to Mr Oto. 'Tiny, perfect, unique.'

At the other end of the phone, Mr Oto clicked his teeth. 'Horn?'

'Yes.'

'Green? Silver?'

'The body is green. Incandescently green. The horn is silver.'

'Bring it to me,' Mr Oto said quietly.

Mr Oto had an appetite for the rare and the weird. Over the years, he had amassed an extraordinary collection of sea creatures: golden carp, green leafy sea-dragons, albino starfish, two-headed crabs. Some of the odder creatures he sold to his wealthy clients, at a huge profit to himself. The alternative medicine market was also extremely profitable: body parts of sea animals were used to remedy everything from heart pain to bad coughs, and black-market trading was always brisk.

Mr Oto had set Pamela up in London on the Battersea side of the river and paid her to trawl the Thames and the nearby North Sea coastline for 'eeby-greebies', as he called them. It was demeaning work. It was immoral. But a mermaid had to eat.

'You want it, Mr Oto,' said Pamela, 'you've got it.'

She had not yet formulated a plan, but how hard could it be? The creature was tiny enough to fit into her hand.

'Fishlock VMW 243, Fishlock VMW 243, this is Saltflat Poutine calling on channel 9. I need you on standby. Over!'

# Chapter 5

Now that she was ten, Thora could travel through cities on her own. One of the first things she loved to do upon arriving in a new place was to head out and buy food. Every country had its own bizarre foods, and often the most disgusting-sounding turned out to be the best-tasting. Seal-flipper pie and poutine in Canada; salt liquorice in Denmark; fried garlic pickles in the United States; bird's-nest soup in China; Violet Crumble and Vegemite in Australia.

Compared with the roasted ants in paper cones they'd bought from a roadside truck in Colombia to munch as they watched the sunset, English food seemed pretty run-of-the-mill. Thora remembered fondly the great bowls of trifle served at the awards banquet after Halla had swum the Bristol Channel. Mounds of whipped cream, fruit and ladyfinger biscuits. Yum! Mr Walters loathed trifle, but he had taught her how to make it, along with many other English dishes such as bubble and squeak, Beef

Wellington, and a full English breakfast of bacon, eggs, kidneys, mushrooms, tomatoes and fried bread. Now Thora wondered what might tickle Mr Walters' fancy and make him eat.

'We need something that will make his mouth water. Something he'll want to gobble up in one bite!'

Cosmo thrust his chin forward as if giving the question deep thought. Shirley released a cloud of greeny-blue sparkles shaped like sausages.

'He does like black pudding,' Thora agreed, a little faintly. The thought of curdled pig blood boiled with chunks of pork fat and stuffed into an edible casing made her feel queasy. 'That might be a bit rich,' she decided, scratching her elbows. 'As would his other favourites, jellied eels, tripe, spotted dick and haggis. But we can't go wrong with a new pot of Patum Peperium and some pear drops.'

Patum Peperium was another name for Gentleman's Relish, a hard greenish-brown paste made from ground anchovies, butter and exotic spices and herbs. Though it smelled disgusting (like the unwashed socks of teenage boys) and had to be wrapped in three layers of waxed paper and sealed in a Tupperware container in the fridge, it was one of Mr Walters' all-time favourites. It was made only in Elsenhame in

Herefordshire and it had been very difficult to obtain when they were abroad.

Then, of course, there was the smelly blue cheese. All gentlemen seemed to like Stilton.

Thora slipped on her backpack and adjusted the straps. She couldn't wait to explore the city by foot. 'I'm off,' she shouted.

Shirley's eyes flashed. To signal her displeasure at being left behind, she emitted into her jug a flourish of steely blue lights that made the water look as if it had goosebumps.

'You can't come touring with me, old Shirl. It's just not freezable. What if I tripped and spilled you on to the street? I'll have a look for a sea-unicorn travel case. If such a thing exists, we'll find it here! Mr Walters says they sell everything in London.'

Shirley flourished some more steely points of light, the equivalent of a sullen *brumpph!* Though she could not speak, she was very expressive, particularly when she was angry.

'Aw, don't be like that,' pleaded Thora. 'We'll go swimming in the harbour when I get back. We'll play one of those Hide and See Weed games you love so much! As long as you promise not to gallop off like you did last time!'

# chapter 6

Thora found Halla propped up on a stool in the kitchen. Halla was very proficient now at getting around inside the *Loki*. When she was tired or when her tail felt dry, she simply slipped into the water through the hole in the floor. Now that she had retired from the underwater swimming circuit, she was much more relaxed. She no longer had to pretend to be something she was not. Although the paparazzi had loved her and splashed her face all over the sports magazines, Halla had never enjoyed public life.

She gave Thora the usual motherly advice about being careful not to show herself as a half-mermaid.

'Cover your scales. Hide your blowhole. Wipe up after yourself. Human beings can be funny about that sort of thing. They'll think you've wet your pants.'

Thora had heard it all before. She knew first-hand about the dreadful things that human beings were capable of doing to mermaids.

What was different this time was that Halla didn't offer to fasten Thora's ponytail at the top of her head. She was too busy grating ginger into Mr Walters' miso soup. Halla had been trying out every recipe she could think of to get Mr Walters to eat. She agreed with Thora that a shopping trip was an excellent idea.

Thora headed along the wharf. The boats moored there were all in tip-top shape. Only the *Loki* was in need of paint! The *Loki* was always in need of paint, Thora reflected. No matter what sort of paint they applied to its hull, after a sea voyage it peeled like strips of bark off a eucalyptus tree.

The *Loki* is just a peely sort of boat, thought Thora fondly.

It was a clear and windless morning, the sky glazed blue as a peacock's egg. A seagull launched itself from a sign that read:

**NO ITINERANTS OR SLEEPING ROUGH.**

It dipped and deposited something soft and white on a woman who sat in a deck chair reading a book on the neighbouring boat, the *Stutch*. She was comfortably plump and wore a poncho patterned with purple stripes, which she used to wipe away the seagull's offering.

'Ahoy!' shouted Thora. The woman smiled shyly and resumed reading.

It was odd to be on land.

After weeks of feeling the swell of the sea beneath her, of watching the golden-green horizon with wind-whipped eyes, of catching teacups before they were tossed to the floor, the solidity of the concrete underfoot made Thora almost city-sick. But she had a mission, and it made her feel very useful and grown-up.

Then again, Mr Walters had always expected Thora to provide the legs in the family, especially in small seaside towns. She had been walking to the shops to buy milk and Polo mints as long as she could remember! When your mother is a mermaid, you have to get your legs into gear early.

As she strolled along Cheyne Walk, the buttery smell of popcorn cut into her thoughts. She stopped and scanned the street for the source. Then she saw a small cinema with glass doors sandwiched between a coffee shop and an Asian grocery store. Her heart fluttered. A woman sat in the booth wearing the slightly bored expression of ticket-sellers the world over. Instinctively, Thora reached for the projectionist's ring that hung around her neck.

The projectionist's ring was magic, but its magic was a little uncertain. Its original owners were the three Greenberg sisters: Thora's granny, Dottie, and great-aunts, Lottie and Flossie. They had given it to Thora with the explanation that 'the magic depends on who wears it'.

So far, the ring had proved itself to be magic in two ways. First, it had helped Thora and her mother escape from the wicked real-estate baron of Grimli-By-The-Sea, Frooty de Mare. Second, it showed films.

Thora had made this surprising discovery one boiling day off the east coast of the Solomon Islands, where the *Loki* had been moored for the week.

As Thora lay on her bed listening to the pinkly sound of ice cubes against the glass of the water jug, she had lifted the projectionist's ring and examined it closely. Then, recalling the old-fashioned equipment at the Greenberg sisters' Allbent Cinema, she got up and hunted through the cabin for the 16-millimetre projector that Mr Walters had once used to watch replays of his favourite cricket matches. She found it in an old windsurfing-slipper box in the kitchen storage cabinet, dusted it off and slipped the ring over the light stem. Miraculously, it fitted.

Tingling from blowhole to tiptoe, Thora untangled the cord and plugged it into a socket in the wall of her bedroom. Then something very odd occurred. Something astonishing, wondrous and exciting.

A black and white image of a couple dancing appeared on the ceiling!

Thora pinched herself, as she sometimes did, to make sure she was not actually asleep and dreaming.

'Better than telly,' she enthused. Shirley agreed wholeheartedly.

Mr Walters found Thora a few hours later, propped up on pillows and staring at the ceiling. He sat on the floor beside her and watched.

'Great Scott!' he exclaimed, one tufty eyebrow raised. 'Impossible!' He examined the ring, the projector, the ceiling. 'Remarkable!'

Halla made a bucket of popcorn and, with Cosmo

and Shirley, they all watched films on the floor of Thora's bedroom for the rest of that night and the next day and the next day after that.

Thora was allowed to use the ring whenever she wanted. Films, they argued, were an important part of her human history. Thora liked the fact that there were no silly adult ratings. She watched them all. As time went by, she learned to control the type of film that the ring would show – though it could still be unpredictable at times.

## Chapter 7

Thora cut an odd figure in her Halla-Skin (her special mermaid-disguising black wetsuit), but nobody took much notice. She liked that about London. People were too polite – or maybe too busy – to stare. It gave her the freedom to really look around, to read the signs. She paused below an enormous billboard to remove a pebble from her windsurfing slipper. Beside a silhouetted image of a man with a croquet mallet were the words:

SOME PEOPLE THINK CROQUET
IS A NICE GAME.
IT'S NOT TRUE.
VISIT THE SNUG CROQUET PALACE.
WATCH CHANNEL SIX.
EXPERIENCE THE DRAMA.

'Mr Walters won't be going there in a hurry,' Thora said aloud, as was her habit. She pretended to thwack a ball with a mallet. 'The most vicious game ever invented, he says!' She looked over at the billboard again. 'Wait a minute! Snug? That's where the Bidets live! What a coincident! I must tell Mr Walters!'

Thora soon forgot all about the shopping she was meant to be doing and drank in the sights. London was the city where Halla had made her first splash in their new life with Mr Walters. She had swum the Thames in record time – a record that still stood. Thora had been a baby then, but when she was older she had read all about it in the newspaper clippings that Mr Walters had saved.

Thora kept her own journal, given to her by Mr Walters, in which she included her thoughts, descriptions of the places they had visited, old film and theatre programmes, postcards, and her own drawings. What would she include this time, from the city of Mary Poppins, Jaffa Cakes, Peter Pan, Princess Di, Harry Potter and Mr Walters' childhood? (In truth, it was hard to imagine Mr Walters as a little boy. When she tried, she could only call into her mind a smaller version of Mr Walters as he was now: thin, dressed in white and walking along the road with his bamboo stick at his own sensible pace.)

Thora found herself at a bus stop. A double-decker bus screeched up beside her and she hopped on, riding on the top floor along the King's Road to Sloane Square. There she took the Tube to Waterloo, climbed a mountain of stairs and hailed a black cab.

In a small shop in Covent Garden Thora bought a pair of second-hand rollerblades and zoomed up Long Acre and through Leicester Square, to the statue of Eros in Piccadilly Circus.

Still, nobody even glanced her way!

Outside Messrs Fortnum & Mason, she admired the doormen in their livery. One of them touched his hat and asked her, politely, to remove her rollerblades. 'We wouldn't want an incident with another shopper.'

Everything looked delicious. And everybody was so formal! Grand! The man who served her was wearing tails and a top hat. The woman who wrapped her parcel was dressed in a black dress with a tall starched white collar.

Carrying in her backpack her Russian Caravan, a year's supply of Gentleman's Relish and a small bag of sugared almonds, Thora hopped back into her rollerblades and whistled over to Hyde Park, stopping to listen to the Flat Earthers rave from their soapboxes. One man waved a black flag, announcing that the end of the world was at hand.

'Which hand?' wondered Thora. 'Which end?'

She popped a few almonds into her mouth and continued her journey, skating past Scot's Corner into Knightsbridge. She pondered whether she should stop at Harrods but remembered it was very expensive and gave it a miss. The Fulham Road was awash with feathery cherry blossom. Pink petals blanketed the parked cars, the postboxes.

As the sun began to set, Thora glanced at her watch. She'd been away for hours and had managed to buy only a few luxuries. She stopped to buy as many basic supplies as she could carry, including a lemon tart and a Stilton, then turned back in the direction of the river.

# Chapter 8

'Fishlock VMW 243, Fishlock VMW 243, this is Saltflat Poutine, Saltflat Poutine, calling on channel 9, over.'

'Saltflat Poutine, this is Fishlock VMW 243, Romeo, change to channel 42, over.'

Miss Fishlock was maddeningly inefficient, a sort of hazy stew of good intentions, but she was devoted to Pamela, could operate the ham radio and, most importantly, she had legs. Two very fat legs that went *swish swish* when she walked. But those fat legs came in handy. They enabled Miss Fishlock to act as Pamela's driver. Having a chauffeur had increased Pamela's mobility substantially! Taxis were very expensive in London.

Pamela had discovered Miss Fishlock at the Aquarium Superstore in Shepherds Bush, where Miss Fishlock had a menial job in the filtration department. It had not taken a lot of coaxing to get her to join Mr Oto's underwater organisation. And, like the best

English people, she did not ask rude questions about Pamela's condition. If she had noticed her boss's tail, she never said a word.

'This is Saltflat Poutine on channel 42. To the wharf in ten. Park on Cheyne Walk. Get the car ready to receive. Over,' said Pamela.

'Fishlock VMW 243. Romeo. Over and out.'

Pamela turned the radio volume down and tossed a few handfuls of economy fish flakes into the tank in her living room. The catfish began its usual squabble with the squid. The albino sea-horse ducked behind a gummy shark and, peeking over, blinked at her impassively with its two pink eyes.

Pamela stuck her tongue out at it and reached for her walking canes. Even with a driver, getting around London required imagination and a lot of effort for a mermaid.

# Chapter 9

On her way back to the *Loki*, Thora came to a row of shops that included a bakery, a butcher and a fishmonger, where she decided to stop and get some supplies for Shirley.

The fishmonger was a stringy woman with a soiled apron over her jumper. She called to Thora in a scratchy voice, 'Special on ghost crabs. C'mon, love, give 'em a look. Ten pounds each. You'll never forget the taste. It'll haunt you for the rest of your life.'

Thora peered at the white and orange flesh in the tray. 'I don't generally eat seafood,' she said. 'Just the occasional cod cheek.'

'Vegetarian?'

'No,' said Thora. 'Mermaid.'

'Ha ha,' said the woman. 'Good one.'

'Do you sell brine shrimp?' asked Thora. 'My sea-unicorn can eat up to 300 a day!'

The woman shook her head. 'This isn't a pet food shop, Ducky. Or should I say Little Mermaid? Ha ha ha.'

The sound of a horn caused Thora to jump on her blades. The Stilton tumbled out of its bag and rolled on to the road, where it was instantly flattened.

A pink station wagon screeched to a halt. It looked out of place against the dark traffic, as if it had driven straight out of Hamleys toy store on Oxford Street. Thora half-expected Barbie to roll down the window and wave.

Then her eyes locked with the driver's.

It took her aback. This was the first person to look her square in the eye all day long! It was a total affront to the senses!

And this driver was no Barbie. More like Barbie's

Texan ranch-handler, an old desert cowboy with a long, almost cone-shaped face creased from a life spent bumping along on a horse, squinting at a blazing sun. A thirsty-looking traveller with chapped lips and, when she looked at Thora over the top of her glasses, eyes that were a sort of white-blue colour. A husky dog's eyes!

'You just squashed my Guardian Angle's Stilton!' said Thora, more surprised than indignant.

'No tragedy there,' snapped the desperado. 'Now, move along.'

A woman's voice? Thora blinked in surprise.

Her gaze shifted to the back of the car. The windows were curtained, as in a hearse, but from where she stood Thora could see spangly reflections of water on the back seat. Thinking it was a trick of light, she leaned forward and saw that the open boot of the car was in fact a large water tank.

'I said move along,' the driver barked. 'Scat!'

'Scat?' repeated Thora, baffled, looking at the ground around her feet. Scat was what Tasmanian-devil droppings were called. 'Where?'

But the car was gone, leaving in its wake the smeared remains of the Stilton on the grey asphalt road.

It smelled terrible.

Thora and Shirley ate a quick supper and, disregarding all the rules about swimming in the dark and immediately after eating, plunged, shrieking, into the water.

The Thames was cold, even for a half-mermaid, but pleasantly so after her long day rollerblading through London. She didn't even mind the smell of diesel oil, or the faint eggy aroma of sewage. Shirley was delighted to be released into the open water, and she performed a complicated sea-unicorn dance that involved somersaults and lunges in a cloud of yellow-green sparkles.

'How about a game of Statues?' suggested Thora.

Statues was one of Thora's favourite childhood games. The point was to twirl your partner around, releasing them into a funny position.

Shirley nodded. She was a bit of a clown and had proven herself to be a much better Statues player than the policeman in Grimli!

Thora gave her a spin and let her go. Shirley swirled around three times, releasing spirals of yellow and pink.

A rather loud voice cut across the water. Two people walking along the wharf were pointing their direction. 'Look at that bright light over there!'

Mr Walters had been adamant that Thora and Shirley weren't to be seen in the river. They both dived deep.

# Chapter 10

Pamela had a number of different systems for tracking her prey, but the good old-fashioned Watch and Wait method had proved successful once again. She'd kept the *Loki* under surveillance since its arrival.

She'd seen a young woman with a camera come and go. Why the camera? Was there something Pamela should know about the strange little family?

She'd watched the gimlet-eyed girl speak with the woman on the neighbouring boat and return hours later on skates, of all things, her backpack heaving with supplies. She had told Miss Fishlock to meet her at the wharf. She should arrive any minute! Then into the aquarium the little green critter would go!

Now, from her discreet position under the wharf, she had her opera glasses trained on the sea-unicorn dancing about the girl near the boat. Their swim in the Thames was a stroke of luck Pamela could only have dreamed of.

Ditto the light show. She'd never known a creature

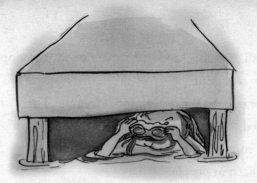

of that size to produce such an astonishing array of colours.

Pamela could hardly wait to hand the sea-unicorn over to Mr Oto. This would be her biggest catch ever. She might even make enough money to retire from sea-snatching and get back to her roots. She wasn't really a fish-rustler. She was an actor. An *artiste*.

Pamela plunged deep and swam towards her prey, transforming herself into what might be described as an utterly charming killer shark.

Shirley's lights had faded and it was too dark and brackish in the water to see where she'd gone. Thora counted to ten and surfaced.

No Shirley.

Worried, she scanned around her, but there was no green sea-unicorn darting this way and that, no scattering of lights to trace in the water.

She dived down and searched the area around the boat. She saw a toothless dogfish, a couple of old

Scottish salmon and an abandoned flip-flop. But Shirley was gone.

Thora swam deeper and deeper. Then, a few hundred metres ahead, she saw Shirley's luminous green form charging through the dark water. Beside her, a flash of purple.

Halla?

Smiling, Thora began to swim after them. They were travelling very fast. But Halla must have seen Thora. Why didn't she stop?

Pamela had thought it would be dead easy to steal the sea-unicorn and make a quick getaway in the car with Miss Fishlock.

But the best-laid plans of mice and mermaids ... How could she have known that the girl could swim so fast?

Or that the vicious little creature would use its horn to bore into her hand? *Ow, the pain!* It smarted more than a stonefish barb. She might even need a rabies shot.

And now the gimlet girl was gaining on them, shouting, 'Wait! Shirley, come back!'

Pamela did not want to be caught green-handed. She let the unicorn go, turned and smiled.

'Where did you learn to swim like that?' she asked winningly.

# chapter 11

It would not be too strong to say that the sight of Pamela's tail held Thora spellbound. It was larger than Halla's and paler – the colour of blackcurrant cordial mixed with milk – but it only held the ghost of a shimmer, the merest touch of phosphorescence. The mermaid's flame-red hair and huge, dark, almost black eyes made Thora think of the ghost crabs she had seen on the fishmonger's slab.

'Your friend and I were just enjoying the most wonderful game of steeplechase,' said the mermaid, holding out her good hand. 'I'm Pamela. What's your name?'

'Thora.'

'A strong name. A Viking name.'

'Yes,' said Thora, blinking hard. 'I'm named after my father, Thor.' She could feel her heart hammering. She took a gulp of water and swallowed. Her throat still felt dry. 'I've never seen another mermaid except for—'

Shirley released a couple of inky blots and darted straight into Thora's outstretched hand.

Thora was transfixed by the mermaid's glamorous, shining face.

Shirley tried to lead her away but Thora ignored her.

'We've been having a marvellous time together!' Pamela said. 'And Thora, you are a truly excellent swimmer for a human, let me tell you. I've seen a lot in my years, but few could keep up the way you did. I was testing you, you see.'

'You were?' asked Thora.

Pamela had a wonderful clear voice with a slight sardine inflection. Its silvery rippliness reminded Thora of her mother's voice.

36

'I'm not nearly as fast as my mother,' she went on. 'She was the open-water swimming champion of the world. She's a mermaid, like you. Only younger.'

It was Pamela's turn to be surprised. 'Your mother?'

'Yes. Halla.'

'The blonde.' Pamela's black eyes flashed.

Shirley poked her silver horn into Thora's arm – not hard enough to hurt, but hard enough to get her attention. Shirley's wings and tail were noticeably less green now. They were, in fact, quite blue. She rattled her mane and tail fiercely.

'Don't mind Shirley,' Thora said apologetically. 'She's just a little hypodermic.'

Pamela fiddled with her earring. 'If your mother is a mermaid, then where is your tail?'

Thora looked down through the water at her legs. 'My father is a human. But he disappeared not long after my parents married. We're not sure where he is. Somewhere interesting, I expect.'

Pamela looked as if she were making some complicated mental calculations. 'Did the Sea Shrew have anything to do with that?' she asked.

Thora laughed nervously. 'You know the Sea Shrew?'

'Of course I do. I'm a mermaid. If you grow up on the sea floor, it's something that can't be avoided. Like rain in London.'

'Why did you come to the World Above?' asked Thora, feeling a little reassured by the matter-of-fact way Pamela was speaking. 'Did you fall in love with a human too?' Perhaps Pamela knew something about her father.

Pamela smoothed her orange hair. 'It's a long story,' she said. 'Maybe I'll tell you about it some time. Right now I must get back to my flat.'

'Your flat? Don't you live in the water?'

'Not if I can help it. I'm extremely sensitive to the cold.' Pamela pointed to a building across from the Chelsea Wharf. 'I live in the Saltworks. I hide my tail, you see. Otherwise I would be discriminated against. And everyone would be trying to sign me up for their freak shows.' Her expression suggested that she was no stranger to suffering.

Thora thought of her mother's experience with Frooty de Mare and shivered.

'You're bleeding,' she said, suddenly noticing Pamela's injured hand. 'Do you want to come back to the *Loki* so we can bandage it? We have a top-rate US Marinade medical kit on the boat.'

'I'm sure you have many wonderful things on your boat,' said Pamela.

'Oh yes, we do! We've collected lots of interesting startlefacts in our world travels.'

'That ring around your neck is *lovely*.'

'The projectionist's ring? Most definitely! It's from Grimli-By-The-Sea. It's magic. It shows films …'

'Films? You might have seen me, then. I was a film

star, you know.'

'No, I didn't,' said Thora cheerfully. 'Is that why you wear so much make-up?'

'Well, no, I …' Pamela's smile faded a little.

'You could come to the *Loki* for tea!' said Thora. 'And I'll show you how it works.'

'How it works?'

'The ring!'

Shirley spat, and rattled her armour again, even more ferociously.

'Oh, I don't like to impose,' said Pamela.

'Oh, but you must,' said Thora. 'You can come tomorrow and meet my mother and my Guardian Angle and Cosmo. We'll have a species reunion. Promise you'll come?'

'Tea time?'

'Perfect.'

Pamela had not forgotten about Miss Fishlock, whom she found parked on Cheyne Walk, waiting obediently for her arrival.

'You can go home. It's all off,' said Pamela, flashing her bleeding palm. 'Until tea time tomorrow.' She wrinkled her nose. 'What's that terrible smell?'

'Stilton,' said Miss Fishlock.

# chapter 12

Halla was reading *A Mermaid's Guide to Organic Sea-Floor Remedies* when Thora burst into the room with news of a new friend named Pamela.

'She lives right here in London!' Thora cried. 'You two will have heaps to talk about!'

'That's nice, darling,' Halla replied. Her hair was wet and her cheeks flushed. She hardly looked up from her book.

'I thought you'd be pleased!' said Thora. 'It's not every day that you meet a mermaid!'

'If it pleases you, it pleases me,' said Halla.

'Well, it does please me. I've invited her for tea tomorrow. She's sooo nice! And very sparkly to speak to! I'm sure Mr Walters will think her smashing. Her tail is a little on the dull side – it seems to have lost a lot of its shimmer – but she's got lovely ghost-crab-coloured hair. Very up-fishmarket!'

Halla looked up. 'Did you say tail?'

Thora crossed her arms and frowned. 'You haven't

heard A WORD I'VE SAID!'

'I have! Someone – some*thing* – with a tail is coming for tea. Here. To the *Loki*! Do you think it was wise to invite her here? Who is she exactly? What is she doing living in London?'

'She was a film star. And she knows the Sea Shrew. Mother, why don't you wear make-up? I admit it looks funny, but … Mother! Mother, you're still not listening!'

Halla marked the page and closed her book. It was hard not to get caught up in Thora's enthusiasm: it would be interesting to meet another mermaid, no question about it. But Halla had more pressing things on her mind.

'Mr Walters' cough is getting worse, Thora. I'm going to have to go to the sea floor to collect some kelp for his flu. I must leave tonight. I'll be away a few days, at least.'

Thora could not hide her disappointment. 'A few days?'

'Maybe less. Anyway, if the mermaid's living around here, I'm sure I'll meet her eventually. We can all get together another time.'

They could hear Mr Walters snoring. Thora tiptoed over and peered into his bedroom. Her heart sank a little. The toast and relish remained untouched on the table by his bed and there was a strong scent of anchovies in the air. Thora took the plate, covered it with an old rain bonnet of Cosmo's and put it in the fridge.

'Do you think the kelp will work?' she asked her mother.

'It's worth a try. Please keep an eye on Mr Walters for me. Don't let him get overtired.'

# Chapter 13

With her two pink canes and a funny hobbly way of walking, Pamela arrived at the *Loki* the next day looking very un-mermaidly. Her hair was pinned up in a French knot; her eyebrows were painted a forgotten shade of orange; and her tail was hidden under a voluminous, rhubarb-coloured silk skirt sporting circular wires that held it out stiffly, giving her the appearance of an ageing Little Bo Peep. She also wore far too much scent.

Thora greeted her with a sneeze. 'You smell a little putrid,' she gasped. 'But you look like … a hundred pounds! Like a film star!'

'You are too kind,' said Pamela.

'Nope, never *too*,' said Thora merrily, helping Pamela to a chair. 'You could easily pass for someone on the cover of a department-store flyer.'

Pamela looked around the cosy cabin, her bright eyes drinking in the odd furnishings and foreign-looking objects. She was surprised by the pictures of film stars and posters, and by the pink walls and lime-green ceiling. There was a curious hole cut into the middle of the floor that had a Plexiglas cover. And a collection of plastic flamingos leaning out of a large Grecian-style urn that made her heart flutter. She loved that shade of pink.

'They're from the hardware store in Grimli,' explained Thora. 'I keep them in stowage when we're sailing so they don't blow away. They're fake.'

'Yes,' said Pamela.

'I'm afraid that neither Shirley nor my mother will be here this afternoon,' said Thora apologetically.

Pamela could not hide her disappointment. 'Oh, how unfortunate. And why is that?'

'My mother has some business of a medical nature,' said Thora.

'And the sea-unicorn?'

'Well, actually,' whispered Thora, pointing in the direction of her bedroom, 'Shirley is home but she is ill-deposed.' In truth, Shirley had flatly refused to see Pamela. Thora had finally given up trying to persuade her.

'Does she always stay in your bedroom?'

'Usually,' said Thora. 'In a well-hydrated, temperature-controlling jug with a generous supply of live brine shrimp to eat.' She paused. 'I am sorry she's not here to talk about the game of chase you two enjoyed yesterday.'

'Never mind,' said Pamela. She held out a gloved

hand to Mr Walters, who had heard the commotion of her arrival and now stood before them in his best Moroccan housecoat and Patagonian hare slippers. He cleared his throat.

'Jack Walters,' he said.

'Pamela P. Poutine,' she replied.

'Poutine?' asked Thora. 'You're kidding!'

'It's French,' said Pamela.

'I *know* it's French! French Canadian! A yummy treat

of chips, gravy and cheese curds! Too greasy for Halla and Mr Walters, but Cosmo and I love it!'

'I can't say I've ever heard of it,' said Pamela with a frown.

'It's a good thing you've got three Ps,' said Thora. 'Otherwise, you'd be Pee Pee for short!'

Pamela pursed her lips. 'Yes,' she continued to Mr Walters. 'I was so delighted to meet this charming girl and her companion in the Thames yesterday. So friendly and open! You can get rather jaded living in a big city like London, where children are heard but never seen.'

'Indeed,' said Mr Walters, coughing into his white hanky.

Pamela asked Mr Walters about himself. She admired the boat. She spoke at length about the dismal weather.

After tea – 'The best I've had since Claridges!' – Thora held up the projectionist's ring.

'Would you like to see how it works?' she asked.

'Why not!' said Pamela.

Thora screwed the ring on to the stem of the old projector. She dimmed the lights and the film went ahead. 'It's a bit of a lottery,' she whispered as the music began. 'We don't always know in advance what film we'll get.'

It was a horror film, but Pamela didn't mind. She watched transfixed right to the final scene.

When they turned the lights back on, Mr Walters

was no longer there. His stomach for horror had weakened and he'd slipped off to his room halfway through the film. Pamela's perfume had given Cosmo a volcanic headache and he'd retired to the roof to get some fresh air into his lungs.

Pamela was alone with Thora. Her head full of the wonders of the projectionist's ring, she questioned Thora closely. She wanted to know everything.

'Show me again how it works.'

Once more Thora dimmed the lights. Immediately a square-jawed actor appeared on the wall. It was an old black and white film starring Montgomery Clift and Elizabeth Taylor.

Pamela sniffed. 'I never thought she was that beautiful. And she grew very fat.'

Then she asked Thora how much she wanted for the ring.

'It's not for sale,' said Thora, surprised. She threaded it once again on to the chain around her neck.

'I see,' said Pamela.

'Yes, exactly. And now that you've seen the ring work its magic, you must sample some of our tail-puckering lemon tart. You must be starving. I am! Horror films always make my stomach growl.'

Thora bounded into the kitchen to prepare their snack. 'I'd tart up the tart with shaving foam, but we've only got aloe vera at the moment and I don't think it's a good combination with lemon!' she called over her shoulder.

When she returned with a tray and a fresh pot of tea, Pamela was sitting with her handbag perched in her lap, looking as if she was about to spring up and go.

'You can't leave yet!' said Thora.

'Watch out!' cried Pamela. 'The walking sticks!'

Too late. Thora stumbled and the two pie portions slipped into Pamela's lap.

'Oops-a-tulip,' Thora sang cheerily.

'Look at the trouble I'm causing,' lamented Pamela, attempting to wipe the lemon filling off her skirt with a lipstick-stained tissue.

'It wasn't your fault!' cried Thora. She dashed to the kitchen for a cloth, dabbed at the mess and then seized Pamela's hand. 'I'm the lemon-tart head here!'

Pamela shrieked and pulled her hand away.

Thora jumped back. 'Did I hurt your hand? I must make it up to you! Take off your glove and let me inspect the damages.'

'Don't be ridiculous. It's nothing. Nothing. Absolutely nothing. Now, I must be off. I've overstayed my welcome already.' Pamela stood up a little unsteadily.

'I can offer you Marmite and toast,' said Thora. 'Or a pear drop?'

Pamela shook her head and kissed Thora French-style, a peck on each cheek. Then, with a *snap* of purse and a *shush* of skirt, she swept out of the *Loki*. Or rather, she tried to sweep out of the *Loki*, but her tail made it difficult.

The sight of the mermaid lurching down the stairs, the wind tearing at her red hair, her skirt flying, filled Thora with admiration. There was something very noble about Pamela, very dramatic. Like a billowing, burning and slightly ragged curtain.

'Thanks for smelling up our evening!' she shouted. 'Come back any time!'

# chapter 14

Despite the little setback with the lemon tart, Thora was in a good mood as she prepared dinner that evening.

'The visit was a rebounding success,' she said to Shirley. 'Mr Walters liked her. I knew he would. He said she was "vivid".' She stopped to scratch her elbows. 'Or maybe it was "livid". Something "ivid", anyway. He must be feeling better. He's reading a book about Babylon.'

Shirley glared at Thora through her jug. Then she turned away and hunched her shoulders. Steely blue lights zig-zagged up around her.

Thora had to sing 'Strangers in the Night' just to get Shirley to turn around.

'I still don't understand why you feel so unfriendly towards Pamela,' she said. 'She's done nothing to you.'

Shirley frowned and twirled, then stabbed her horn into a tiny water cactus on the bottom of the water jug.

'What are you doing?' Thora cried.

Shirley lifted her wings. She wanted to be picked up.

Once in Thora's hand, she poked her horn into Thora's palm. Then she pointed towards the window.

'Outside?'

Shirley nodded.

'The wharf? The bridge?'

Shirley shook her head. She wagged her tail, fluttered her eyelashes and produced a series of tiny red-orange sparkles that were the same colour as Pamela's hair.

'Pamela?'

Shirley nodded and pressed the tip of her horn into Thora's palm again.

'Ouch!' cried Thora, examining her palm. 'You're obviously trying to make a point, Shirl. Did you poke Pamela, too?'

Shirley gave her a mysterious look.

'Either you did or you didn't.'

Shirley looked away. Thora plopped her back into the water jug and put her hands on her hips.

'No wonder she left in a hurry. Poor Pamela! How could you? You just don't do that to a guest. It doesn't matter if they're not your cup of Russian Caravan. It's anti-sociable! It's un-syllabised! You can come to her place with me tomorrow to apologise. I'll carry you over in a zip-lock freezer bag.'

Shirley shook her head.

'She might never come here again.'

Shirley began to dance for joy. A beautiful flourish of blue and green lights swirled around her.

'Shirley!'

# Chapter 15

Thora woke late the next morning to the hammering of rain on the roof. She stretched and looked at her clock. It was almost 10 a.m., which was surprising, because it was still dark in her room.

'Good morning, Shirl,' she said. 'Isn't it interesting that we always sleep late when it rains? Mr Walters says it's due to the barren metric pressure.'

Shirley tucked her chin into her chest and closed her eyes.

'You're loitering a bit palely this morning! Ready to go and apologise to Pamela yet?'

Shirley shook her head.

Thora had to switch on the light to get dressed.

'It's a little like starting your day in reverse: getting up in the dark, dressing for the day in the evening. Maybe we should have dinner for breakfast. A little round of rump steak with mash and peas would go down well this morning!'

Through the window she could see the rain gusting down. With a shiver, she pulled on a blue alpaca jumper, given to her by a Peruvian schoolgirl after Halla swam Lake Titicaca. It was soft and cosy though three of the original five buttons had fallen off.

Thora wondered if her mother was back from her kelp-collecting mission yet. She longed to tell her about Pamela's visit.

In the living room, Thora discovered Cosmo twirling a pink stick on the tip of his beak. He wasn't as dextrous as the Girl Guide majorettes that Thora had seen at the New Year's Orange Bowl Parade in Miami, but he could manage a basic spin.

Thora rustled up her first meal of the day. She grilled a small round of steak, fried some mushrooms in garlic and butter, and heated up a scoop of leftover mashed potatoes. There were no peas, so she settled for diced green apple. Then she carried a tray into Mr Walters' bedroom.

'We're having a backwards day,' she said. 'I thought you might like some of my dinner for breakfast!'

Mr Walters looked quite well, though he declined Thora's offer to share her steak and requested a pot of tea instead. 'Maybe just a PG Tips, nothing fancy.'

'You must be feeling better,' said Thora.

'A bit, yes,' responded Mr Walters.

He joined Thora in the kitchen. As she ate, he told her about his university days at Oxford and how he'd been part of the Hysteron-Proteron Club, whose members lived their days in reverse.

'Excellent! Let's join!' Thora pulled out Scrabble, a game usually reserved for evenings. 'I'm going to visit Pamela when we're finished,' she said. 'I'm so looking forward to seeing her again. Shirley's been terribly rude to her. I'm going to go and make our apologies. Shirley refuses to come. 'You liked Pamela, didn't you, Mr Walters?'

Mr Walters looked out through the window at the falling rain. 'I've never really been partial to redheads.'

'Well, she can't help the colour of her hair,' said Thora.

'Oh, I expect she can,' Mr Walters replied.

By the time the game of Scrabble wad over, the rain had eased up, but the sky had taken on a grey-purple colour that reminded Thora of cold boiled potatoes.

Well, she wasn't going to be caught in another

downpour. She tucked the projectionist's ring into her Halla-Skin, slipped on a yellow macintosh and stepped into one of the pairs of size 6 windsurfing slippers scattered around the houseboat. She found an old umbrella, but it was broken from the mini-hurricane they'd encountered in the Bay of Biscay. After visiting Pamela, she'd try to buy another. You couldn't hope to stay dry in London without a working brolly.

'I can't take you with me today, Cosmo. Your tail would make it too difficult for you to travel in reverse.'

Cosmo tried walking backwards and immediately bumped into the Turkish footstool and fell over.

Out on the wharf, the air smelled of wet wood and salt and diesel oil – a familiar, earthy smell that came

to all seaports around the world after rain. Thora
turned and walked backwards. No cheating allowed!

Up on the bridge, the cars travelled with their
headlights on. The pavement was spattered white and
grey with pigeon droppings and sodden bits of litter.
At the Saltworks Luxury Flats, Thora climbed the stairs
to two wide glass doors gilded with chipped patterns
of painted ivy and pressed the intercom button next to
Pamela's name. But there was no response.

# chapter 16

Through her rain-streaked living-room window, Pamela watched Thora come and go, walking backwards each way! What an odd creature. Despite being dressed like a deep-sea fisherman, the girl behaved like a gymnast or a dancer, springy-footed and elastic in her movements and, well, annoyingly *happy*. Pamela felt an unexpected sadness sweep through her – a longing for her glory days when she was young and beautiful and light of tail. Never in her life had she known what it was like to walk – forwards *or* backwards – on two legs through London.

'Miss Fishlock,' she called out, 'is my bath ready yet?'

'Yes.' Miss Fishlock came into the room, drying her hands with a small tea towel. 'I'll take over here,' she said. 'You go and have a good soak.'

Pamela passed her assistant the pink opera glasses. 'The girl has headed out.'

'Thora? Excellent.'

'And the mother is still away. Only the old geezer and the peacock in the boat now.'

'And the sea-unicorn.'

'And the sea-unicorn,' said Pamela impatiently.

When Miss Fishlock was installed at the living-room window, Pamela lurched on her canes to the bathroom, undressed and hauled herself into the tub.

Her hand started to sting where the wretched little creature had stabbed her. But the temperature of the water was perfect, cool without being cold, and scented with the Japanese seaweed that Miss Fishlock had pinched from the Asian grocery store. Pamela reached for the salt scrub. None left.

Times were tough for Pamela.

It had been twenty-five years since she'd left the ocean floor, incurring the wrath of the Sea Shrew. She wasn't content with being a big mermaid in a small

pond. For twenty-five years she had struggled to make a go of it in a society where what mattered was legs, legs, legs. Legs and loot. Her attempts to break into film had taught her about the cruelty of human beings. She'd been treated like a freak, cast in tacky television ads, paid poorly and sacked before she'd had a chance to prove herself. It was desperation thathad forced her to turn to a life of petty crime – living beside the docks, forever fearful of returning to the coral reefs of her childhood, and still hoping to be discovered.

Mr Oto had discovered her, all right. As well as being a millionaire collector, he was a successful film producer in Kabukiwood. It was Mr Oto who had cast Pamela in *Neptune's Stepsister*. She had shown talent in the mouth-to-mouth resuscitation scene, but it was her demand for a body double that had caused the director to sack her. She was not being unreasonable! The scene had demanded that she be thrown into a pit with two live alligators!

The film work dried up. Just like that. And feeling a little bit sorry for Pamela, Mr Oto had come to an arrangement with her. Would she be willing to search the sea for unusual animals? It paid 'very handsomely'.

Reluctantly, Pamela agreed. But she never quite abandoned her teenage dream. And now, with the extremely valuable sea-unicorn within her grasp, it appeared that the future was opening up again. It was not the unicorn but the money that she really wanted. Money was freedom.

She'd hand Shirley over. Get her money. Get her tail out of this demeaning job. She never wanted to see another freaky sea creature. She was sick of them.

She shut her eyes and massaged her lids. She'd learned from the telly that facial massage could make you look younger *and* relieve headaches.

Mr Oto had said he would fly from Tokyo to London on his private jet to collect the sea-unicorn. But first he wanted the call confirming that she had captured it.

From the other room, she heard Miss Fishlock's excited voice.

'They're leaving, Pamela. Come quickly!'

Pamela galumphed out of the bath, flung on her fluffy white robe and made her way to the window. 'They?'

'The old man and the peacock.'

'Give me the glasses.'

On the wharf she saw an extremely tall figure dressed in white making its way down Cheyne Walk. The flash of blue at his feet suggested that the peacock was with him.

Pamela pressed the glasses back into Miss Fishlock's hand. 'This is going to be easier than I thought,' she said. A huge smile spread across her face. 'It's time,' she said. 'Go and steal the jug.'

# Chapter 17

Mr Walters had not been out for a walk since arriving in London, and had started to feel a little claustrophobic, especially since watching that dreadful horror film last night. Halla would get cross with him for going out in the damp weather, but he couldn't lie about in bed all day every day. He covered his mouth with his hanky, and he and Cosmo headed off in the direction of Cheyne Walk. He would visit the café he'd once frequented with Imogen.

He wondered what Imogen would have made of Pamela; the thought of them all sitting down to tea and crumpets made him chuckle. Imogen had never been very good at hiding her true feelings. She too had disliked horror films.

It struck him suddenly that the projectionist's ring had never before shown a horror film. Perhaps it chose its audience! Perhaps it knew something that they didn't!

It did not take long for Mr Walters and Cosmo to

reach the café. It had been converted into a newsagency, a fact that might have saddened Mr Walters had he not been such an avid newspaper reader. The bell on the door sounded as he pushed it open and entered the shop.

He stopped dead in his tracks when he read the *Evening Standard*'s headline.

# chapter 18

Thora's hair was soaked and water was running down the inside of her macintosh collar. When the first shop she'd tried was sold out of umbrellas, she'd decided to do without. She was half-mermaid, after all, and not that fussed about the wet!

She hopped on a bus and sat back to front on the seat, then walked backwards through the rain to the Tate Gallery and requested a ticket to start at the end. The ticket-seller refused. But nobody stopped her from walking through the gallery backwards, examining the pictures from an upside-down position.

Thora found that for many paintings it didn't much matter if you looked at them forwards or backwards, on your feet or on your head. For some reason, this was a thrilling discovery to make.

At the Tate, people seemed to step aside just so she, Grebneerg Aroht, aged ten and three-quarters, could reverse through her day. Not even the woman in the gallery café seemed surprised when Thora requested a bowl of porridge and two slices of toast with Marmite for afternoon tea. Yes, London was a great city!

# Chapter 19

Pamela tightened the sash on her white robe and ran her fingers along the glass of the Belvedere aquarium.

She was tingling, top to tail. 'My pets,' she said to the dozen or so creatures in the tank, 'you will soon be receiving a special guest. I would like you to treat her well. She won't be staying long! She's on her way to Tokyo!' Pamela tossed them some dried fish-food flakes and turned to peer triumphantly out of the living-room window.

She wished she had not lent the opera glasses to Miss Fishlock. Without them it was difficult to make out the shapes in the harbour. Never mind. With luck, Miss Fishlock would be returning in less than an hour. Pamela crossed her fingers and turned up the volume on the ham radio. If anything went wrong, Miss Fishlock would use the radio in the *Loki*.

Then the phone rang.

'Miss Pamela? This is Lee.'

'Lee?'

'Mr Oto's secretary. Mr Oto would like to know if you have captured the green sea-unicorn yet.'

Pamela ran her fingers through her hair and smiled into the phone. 'Lee, the unicorn is on her way now. In a matter of minutes, she will be right here before me. I would urge Mr Oto to board his jet now.'

'Mr Oto is very excited. But he would like you first to have the creature in your hand before he will fly. Please call to confirm, yes?'

Pamela felt annoyed, but she didn't let on. 'Of course, Lee. I'll call you back in a few minutes.'

Pamela returned to the window. A fog was rolling in over the harbour, reducing visibility further. She strained to make out the familiar shape of the *Loki* across the water.

But she couldn't see it. This was odd. Perhaps her eyes were playing tricks on her. She felt the beginnings of a headache pulsing in her temples.

Then the ham radio cut into her thoughts with a sound like a fart.

'Saltflat Poutine, this is Fishlock VMW 243. Mayday! Mayday! Delta Echo! Charlie Quebec! Oh, bother. HELP!'

# Chapter 20

Thora found it was necessary to walk backwards all the way home. The wind was blowing so strongly that it gave her an earache, but by turning around, she could keep her face and ears out of the wind. And watch the fog rolling in over the dull grey surface of the river.

She was worried about Mr Walters. He'd be wondering where she was by now. But the evening rush hour was underway and she couldn't travel home as fast as she would have liked. The cars sat bumper to bumper, only their windscreen wipers moving. Everyone in a hurry, going nowhere.

No drivers were making any concessions for pedestrians or wet half-mermaids. Thora tried in vain to get the drivers' attention by shouting, singing, waving and knocking. Sometimes a girl wanted a little eye contact, preferably with someone who was not a female desperado! Finally, she hopped up on to the bonnet of the nearest car and used the others as stepping stones to cross the street. FOUR–THREE–TWO–ONE!

She landed on the pavement on the other side of the street with a *smuch*!

Nobody honked a horn or called after her. Perhaps they were used to it. Or maybe they couldn't see her in the fog.

It was thickening now, gaining a billowy grey weight as it absorbed the evening's shadows. 'A real split-pea supper,' said Thora. It was a relief to be drawing closer to home, but it was becoming harder to see the familiar landmarks. She walked slowly, keeping the traffic noises to the right.

Outside a newsagency on Cheyne Walk, she passed a bench spread with newspapers and, poking from under the bench, a seagull that looked smudged in the fog, like a puff of smoke with a beak. What was that noise? Snoring? She drew closer. Underneath the newspaper a man was talking to himself. An itinerary sleeping rough?

'Lionel!' said the man. 'Hello, dear chap. Such a long time! I'm sorry I missed you. I wanted to congratulate you on what was, in every respect, a great innings!'

Thora knew that voice. She knew it like the scales on her shins. She lifted the paper. 'Mr Walters!' she cried.

He opened his eyes. 'My dear girl! I was having the most extraordinary dream about the Duke of Snug!'

Cosmo stepped out of the fog.

'Cosmo! Mr Walters, what are you two *doing* out here? Your poor old cold! Are you all right?'

Mr Walters knees cracked like poppadoms as he stood up. He brushed himself off, folded up the papers and tucked them under his arm. His lips were drained of colour and his steps unsteady. 'I can hardly believe it,' he said.

'What is it, Mr Walters? What's wrong?'

Mr Walters unfolded the damp newspaper and pointed a long index finger at another headline.

**THE GREAT DUKE OF SNUG DIES. HIS SON, LORD BIDET, TO ASSUME TITLE.**

'Your friend? Oh, Mr Walters, I'm so sorry!'

'Lionel was a great man,' said Mr Walters with a wobble in his voice. 'I must call Jerome. My godson.'

Thora held Mr Walters' arm as they made their way down the slippery steps to Chelsea Wharf. They walked slowly, with Cosmo trailing, keeping the slurping water noises to their left. But when they came to where Thora thought the *Loki* ought to be moored, all she could see was someone's head, peeping over the dock.

'Who's there?' came a voice.

'Is that you, Mother?' said Thora. She let go of Mr Walters and rushed over to the water's edge. 'Where is the *Loki*?'

Halla shook her head. 'I was hoping that you could answer that question.' Then she buried her face in her hands.

# chapter 21

'Fishlock VMW 243, this is Saltflat Poutine calling on channel 42, come in, over.'

'Romeo. How do I stop this thing?'

'Stop what thing?' said Pamela. 'What are you talking about? Are you in the car? Over.'

'No, I'm … I'm in the fog. I didn't …' Miss Fishlock's words were a jumble. 'I tried this red button here and this lever but nothing is stopping it, slowing it down! Roger. Over.'

'Fishlock, get a grip! Where are you? Do you have it? Do you have it? Over.'

'I'm driving it! But I'm about to—'

'Driving what?'

'The *Loki*!'

'What are you doing that for?'

'You told me to.'

'I did not.'

'But you said to steal the tug.'

Pamela felt all the blood drain out of her face and pool in her tail.

'You took the BOAT? The *LOKI*?'

She was furious. Miss Fishlock had blown it. Again.

'I said take the JUG, you idiotic goose, not the TUG!'

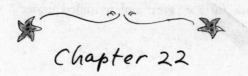

# Chapter 22

'What do you mean?' asked Thora. 'I don't understand!' She repeated, 'Where is the *Loki*?'

'I returned an hour ago with *that*,' said Halla, pointing pitifully to a mound of kelp on the wharf. 'The boat wasn't here. I swam around the harbour. Nothing. I hoped that you two had taken her for a ride. It was the only explanation that made sense. Unless ...'

'Unless she was stolen,' said Mr Walters, suddenly looking very old.

'But Shirley was on board!' said Thora. Then Mr Walters' words registered. 'Stolen? Do you really think ...? How? Who? We must find the *Loki*! We must find Shirley!' She looked around. 'Don't just stand there! Isn't there *something* we can do?'

Mr Walters said nothing, but his look confirmed what Thora was thinking.

The terrible events pressed down on them.

In the water below, Halla's teeth were chattering.

Thora, too, felt herself growing cold; she rubbed her hands together and stamped her feet as she searched the river for signs of Shirley – a trail of sparkly lights, a flash of green or yellow or pink – but all she saw was the dark surface, grey and wrinkled under a starless sky.

## STOLEN, SMASHED AND SUNK

Yesterday, at approximately 2.04 p.m. GMT, a mid-sized houseboat, the *Loki*, belonging to Mr Jack Walters, was stolen from its mooring at Chelsea Wharf. The thief was reported to be driving erratically. One witness, an American kayaker who claims to have avoided a collision by a mere couple of metres, said that the driver was probably a man but might have been a woman.

'I was very scared.'

After leaving Chelsea Wharf, the thief appears to have collided headlong into Albert Bridge. It is believed the boat was exceeding the speed limit at the time of the accident. There is no known motive for the crime. Police believe the driver escaped on foot.

Any witnesses to the crime are asked to contact the Thames River Police immediately.

# chapter 23

Thora and Mr Walters read the newspaper article in the kitchen of the *Stutch* while its owner, Elin, served them hot Horlicks. Cosmo sat gloomily at Mr Walters' feet. Halla was keeping a low profile under the jetty near where the *Loki* had been moored. She was not in the mood to answer questions about her tail.

The article made no mention of a sea-unicorn. Thora and Mr Walters sipped their drinks in silence, thinking about dear little Shirley.

Why anyone would want to steal the *Loki* was a question they couldn't answer. Shirley was another matter. They all knew she was rare, but only Mr Walters had realised her commercial value.

'Do you think the thief stole her? Do you think she's hurt, or …' Thora could not finish the question.

Mr Walters put his arm around Thora. 'Underneath that princess exterior, Shirley is an empress! Just remember, Thora, she has survived abandonment, bullying and a whirlpool in the South China Sea. I am quite certain she can survive a boatwreck in the Thames.'

Thora went outside to tell Halla that the *Loki* had been found.

Halla and Thora decided to swim along the river to take a look at the *Loki* and see what sort of condition she was in. It was a terrible thought, but perhaps Shirley had been trapped inside the boat. Or at least it would let them narrow down their search for her. Thora also wanted to find her journal.

Mr Walters forbade them to go near the boat until midnight. He was afraid that the police would get suspicious. Halla could end up at some sort of Sea World, and Thora in a foster family. This had already happened to her back in Grimli.

Mr Walters felt that the best course of action was to accept Elin's offer of accommodation until the river police had finished investigating the theft. If the *Loki* was salvageable, the family would get it repaired. If it was not ... well, they would crash into that bridge when they had to.

'Bidet here.'

Mr Walters cleared his throat. 'Jerome, I dreamed about your father last night,' he said. 'He was looking rather well, all things considered.'

'Mr Walters? Can it be? Is it possible? Tell me I'm not dreaming! It's been years!'

'You're not dreaming. It's the old fossil who tried to teach you how to swing a cricket bat.'

'The old fossil who utterly, miserably, pathetically failed to do so! How are you? Happy does not do it justice. I'm ecstatic to hear your voice, delighted, elated, exhilarated … and …'

'Bowled over?' offered Mr Walters.

Jerome paused. 'You heard the news?'

'Jerome – I am so sorry,' said Mr Walters.

'It's been tough,' said Jerome, his voice cracking. 'I wasn't ready to let him go. But then again, one never is. Now, are you all right? How is your health? Where are you? What are you doing?'

Mr Walters took a deep breath and told his godson everything.

Jerome was appalled by the unfortunate turn of events. 'Listen, while your boat is being repaired, you must bring everyone up to the country. Get them out of wretched London. We'll toast Dad and I can meet your charges. You can stay in the folly out the back of the house – we'll clear out all of Dad's old stuff.'

'There's just one thing, Jerome, that I haven't mentioned.'

'Yes?'

'Halla is ... well, she doesn't have the use of her legs.'

Jerome was unfazed. He had been in a wheelchair for almost a decade and it had opened his eyes to a new world. He knew many people who 'did not have the use of their legs'. It was not so unusual, really.

'Righty-o,' said Jerome. 'We've got a fleet of wheelchairs here, if she needs one.'

'That might be useful,' said Mr Walters.

'Does she have any special requirements?'

'Yes,' said Mr Walters. 'There are water needs.'

'Water needs? How mysterious! Hydrotherapy or something? Blandina is always trying to get me to into – what are they called? Aqua-aerobics classes? Well, there's the lake, as you know. But it needs dredging. A bit overgrown for swimming.'

Mr Walters decided to wait until they got to Snug before telling Jerome the full truth about Halla. Some information is best passed on in person.

'It will do Louella a world of good to have some company at this difficult time,' Jerome went on. 'She would be a similar age to your Thora, wouldn't she? Ten? Eleven? It's appalling. I don't even know my own daughter's age!'

Mr Walters smiled. Jerome had not changed.

'You'll find we've come down a peg or two. I can't supply you with a driver any more. But Milton loves an excuse to nip into London. He can collect you in the Rolls. It's a bit beaten up, but the car's my pride and joy.'

Before ringing off, they agreed that Milton would collect Mr Walters and his family from the wharf in two days' time.

Plus ⊕ and Minus ⊖
news about the Loki.

First the minus:

- No shirley...
- Most personal things (Mr Walters' precious books) too wet to save
- Beds, cushions and all other furnacings ruined.
- Boat doctor says he needs six MONTHS (OR maybe more!) to repair Loki. (He offered to repair the hole in living room floor but Mr W told him to leave it alone.)
- We have no home we can call our own.
- Feel very... desolated. Mr W out of breath. Says burglary has dimmed his view of humankind.

Now for the 'PLUS!'

- The Loki will survive.

- Also ... I found my journal floating in my bedroom above the dressing table. It was in PEPPERMINT condition (how else could I be writing in it now?) Am so happy I zippered the zipper on the ZIP-LOCK bag.

- Dishes, teacups, wetsuits, etc are wet but will prevail.

- Also, so will windsurf slippers, plastic comb and most wooden things such as bookshelves, kitchen table, etc.

- Mr Walters' friends in the country have invited us to stay with them while the Loki is getting fixed.

Jerome Bidet has an eleven-year-old daughter, Louella.

Mr Walters has bought a flowered Thai sarong for Mother from Portobello Road market.

The sarong will hide Mother's tail while we make the journey in the car to Snugshire.

- I have posted signs about Shirley around Chelsea & Chelsea Wharf.
(Elia says people will tear them down!)

# Missing in Action
## 1 Sea-horse unicorn

name: Shirley
age: 3
size: 2 inches
wt: 370 grams
colour: Green (bright)

Distinguishing characters:
– silver horn, proud, good
appetite (eats shrimp brine)
PLEASE CONTACT POLICE IF YOU
KNOW, SEE OR HEAR anything
about SHIRLEY'S WHIRLABOUTS

Thankyou,
Sincerely,
Thora Greenberg age 10¾.

# Chapter 24

Mr Walters had known the old Duke, Lionel, for over fifty years. Their wives had been school chums. Though it sounds rather old-fashioned, the two women had considered themselves *bosom friends*. Nothing changed after Imogen's marriage to Mr Walters. Mr Walters and Mrs Walters were embraced as family and given an open invitation to Snug House. How many happy hours the couples had spent playing cricket on the lawns, fishing for trout, lazing with books in Mexican hammocks, munching crisps and sipping Pimm's!

When Mr Walters' work forced him to travel, Mrs Walters would stay at Snug House. She did not have children of her own and was very attached to her best friend's only child Jerome, her godson.

The Duke of Snug, or Len to his friends, considered himself something of an amateur William Beebe (the American ocean explorer and author). Lionel was passionate about his replica of Beebe's and Barton's

Bathysphere, an underwater exploration chamber, which he had bought at auction in New York in the early 1960s and had shipped to Snugshire. For almost forty years, Lionel had tinkered with the Bathysphere in the hope of one day taking it out to Nonsuch Island in Bermuda and seeing for himself the underwater marvels Beebe had described in his many books.

But Lionel's duties at Snug House kept him so busy that it never happened. The Bathysphere became a bit of an embarrassment to the Duchess, who did not take her husband's passion for it very seriously. Eventually, Lionel decided to satisfy his love of the sea by collecting marine curios.

Mr Walters had written to the Bidets about his new family, and had spoken on the phone to Lionel and Jerome. The Bidets knew of Halla's success as an open-water swimmer; knew Mr Walters had taken custody of Halla's daughter, Thora. But they did not know that Halla was a mermaid, or that her daughter had a blowhole and purple scales on her shins. Nor did they know anything about her husband Thor.

Now Len was dead.

It had not been easy for Mr Walters to read his friend's obituary.

# Chapter 25

They were hard to miss – Mr Walters with his trilby hat and slightly sooty cricket whites, Thora in her wetsuit with her fountain spray of red-brown hair falling into her eyes, Halla wrapped from her waist to the floor in a bright orange sarong, and finally the electric-blue peacock with his metre-long tail. Despite the vivid colours and odd clothing, they looked worn out – like travelling circus performers who had given their all and were unsure of what the future held.

While they waited for Milton, Mr Walters sketched out the Bidet family tree. 'Families can get complicated,' he said.

Thora examined the diagram. 'Families should stay together!' she announced.

'They should,' agreed Halla, 'but it isn't always possible.'

'There he is!' cried Mr Walters, pointing his bamboo walking stick at an approaching car.

# The Bidet family tree

1. The Duke, Lionel Bidet (deceased)
2. The Duchess (deceased)
3. Jerome - lizard expert
   uses wheelchair
   The new Duke
4. Louella Bidet, age 11 - daughter
   of Jerome

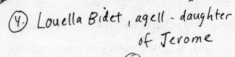

3a. Blandina - Second wife of Jerome.
    The new Duchess

3b. Professor - Ex wife of Jerome
    Louella's mother. Mr Walters
    can't recall her name.

Milton waggled his eyebrows when he saw the walking cane and the awkward way Halla used it.

'Do you need some help?' he asked politely. 'I could carry you out to the car.'

'Oh, no,' said Halla. Her face flooded with relief as she tumbled into the spacious back seat.

Thora scrambled in beside her. The cream-coloured leather upholstery crackled as she drew her knees up and hugged them.

From the front, Mr Walters passed Halla a wad of newspapers which, Milton observed through his rear-view mirror, were dripping wet. To his astonishment, she flattened them out and began to stuff them, unread, under her skirt.

Milton blushed and averted his eyes and off they went.

# chapter 26

Pamela P. Poutine was a mess.

On the night of the accident, while she was scouring the wrecked *Loki* and surrounding area for signs of her assistant and the green sea-unicorn, somebody had broken into her flat and stolen her valuable collection of sea creatures.

That same night, the shrimp-pink station wagon had disappeared.

Pamela had set herself up by the big window of her flat with her sparkly pink opera glasses and watched the movements of Thora, Mr Walters and Cosmo from their new base in a boat called the *Stutch*. But it had not been long before they'd all headed off in a dilapidated Rolls-Royce – even the mermaid. Without transport or money, there'd been no way of following them.

To cap it all, Miss Fishlock had fallen out of contact.

Perhaps she'd drowned in the boat accident, or received a blow on the head that had given her amnesia?

Or, more likely, perhaps Miss Fishlock was somewhere out there in London. But with or without Shirley was the question.

Either way, the betrayal was monstrous.

And it didn't help that Mr Oto's secretary was brushing her off now.

'The Great Oto will speak to you when and *if* you produce the green sea-unicorn. Goodbye, Miss Pamela.'

# Chapter 27

Milton was a pleasant man, neither young nor old, with a grizzle of rust-coloured hair and an inky-blue tattoo of a shark on his arm. A furry green sea-horse with bulging marble eyes dangled from his rear-view mirror. He'd once been captain of a chartered yacht in Bermuda, he told them, but a bad ear infection had rendered him prone to seasickness.

'Driving is easier on my gut,' he said, 'though I miss the sea critters!' He switched on a classical music station and lapsed into companionable silence.

The traffic on the M25 was light. After an hour or so, the road grew leafy, twisting into a series of green hills that eventually gave way to flatter tracts of land dotted with rustic cottages and sheep. It felt like a continent away from the grind and grey of London.

'With the *Loki* gone, we can travel light from now on,' said Mr Walters. 'That's something, at least.'

Halla shivered and looked down through the damp orange cotton of her sarong at the football scores.

Cosmo sighed and nestled his head in Mr Walters' lap.

'Come on, folks. It's not the end of the world. The umpire has called her down for a while. *But not forever,*' Mr Walters said. Soon he was snoring gently, his hat tipped over his eyes, his mouth slightly open.

In the back seat, Thora felt a strange sense of unreality. She had never really lived away from the sea and she was not sure she was going to like it. An image kept floating into her mind of Shirley turning up at the dock where the *Loki* had been moored. Had they done everything they could to find her? Mr Walters had reported her missing. Halla and Thora had scoured the area around the *Loki* both nights. Their only hope was that someone would read one of the signs, contact the police and return Shirley to them.

And what about all of the family's lost treasures? Thora made a mental list of her favourite things – objects she would never see again:

- the snowy owl carved from caribou antlers
- the Turkish footstool
- her saggy but comfortable bed
- the flounder-shaped oven mitt
- the angel food cake tin
- the kettle that sang 'Oh Susannah'
- the six pink flamingos
- the framed poster for *Gone with the Wind*
- her father Thor's signed photographs of Ava Gardner and Greta Garbo.

She stared out the window at the flowing grey asphalt. She felt cold and tired and racked by the sort of dizziness that might come from living a day in reverse. But she wasn't walking backwards this time, or standing on her head. No, she was facing forwards in a stranger's car, hurtling towards an unknown house, family and future without her dear little sea-unicorn. Her little Shirley.

She had lost much of what she knew and loved and it made her feel exposed, stripped down – like a scribbly gum after it sheds its outer layer.

At least she'd found her journal.

And she still had her precious projectionist's ring.

She turned the ring over in her hand. *To the Marriage of Earth and Sea*, said the inscription. Half of land. Half of sea.

Half dry. Half wet. Human and mermaid. Me. Thora Greenberg.

The car slowed down.

'Welcome to Snug House,' Milton announced.

## Chapter 28

As they passed through the grand gates of the Bidet estate, Thora perked up.

At the end of a long avenue of lime trees, they drove under a white arch densely dotted with gooseberries, and into the main courtyard.

Mr Walters sighed as if meeting an old friend.

Thora whistled.

Halla licked her parched lips.

Milton followed the slow curve of the driveway. On either side of the house the lawn stretched for several hundred metres, crew-cut short, lemon-lime in colour and hedged with tall, rather unruly holly and blackberry bushes. To the right was a group of cherry trees, huddling like teenage girls and twittering pink and white with the last bits of May blossom. To the left grew mulberry trees, horse chestnuts and sycamores.

Further back from the house they could see evidence of construction – piles of mud, gravel and workmen's

95

bric-à-brac. A large section of lawn was cordoned off and flagged as a no-entry zone. A site sign read:

CROQUET COURTS
KEEP OUT

A small decorative garden of roses and white tulips bordered the house. Snug House itself was enormous, constructed out of custard-coloured stone, patterned with green and white lichen and lassooed with creeping vines. The wide flight of steps at the front was flanked by empty-eyed statues and weathered Greek urns that reminded Thora of some she had seen in Thessaloníki.

Overall, the effect of the house was grand but somehow slightly neglected.

'Where's the folly?' asked Thora.

'Out the back,' said Mr Walters.

'I need water,' said Halla weakly from the foot of the steps. She was not accustomed to using a walking stick, or to moving any sort of distance on land, and it showed on her face.

Mr Walters turned to the driver. 'Milton, could we

trouble you to carry this good woman to the grotto out behind the folly for a quick dip?'

'A dip?' Milton look mystified.

'A swim in the grotto – you know, to freshen up.'

'There'd be plenty of hot water in the house, I reckon, if madam would prefer a nice bath. The grotto is rather … well, grotty!'

'I don't mind grotty,' said Halla weakly.

'OK, then,' he said, lifting her up. 'Actually, I sometimes do this for Lord Bidet – the Duke.'

'You do?' asked Mr Walters.

'Well, carry him, I mean. He doesn't tend to swim in the lake.'

Milton took Halla off to the grotto, and the rest of them climbed the grand flight of steps.

Thora gave Cosmo a little pat on the head then pressed the front doorbell.

# Chapter 29

The door swung open to reveal a frowning girl, about eleven years old, carrying a suitcase. She was breathing hard as if she'd been running. She was small and precise-looking, with quick hazel eyes and a pair of black-framed spectacles sitting crookedly on her little upturned nose.

'You must be Louella,' said Mr Walters. 'Let me introduce everybody.'

Louella's eyes darted from Thora to Mr Walters to Cosmo. Then, in a voice so dry it made Thora feel thirsty, she said, 'Daddy told me you've all lost your home. I do extend my condolences. You, too, know what it is

like to be … displaced. Mr Walters will be staying upstairs. You'll be living in the folly. My old Think House. Perhaps the bird – what's his name? Daddy couldn't remember – can stay outside. I don't want droppings everywhere.'

'Cosmo is toilet-trained,' said Thora indignantly.

'Then he would be a very unusual peacock. I've read all about them. Their droppings smell particularly vile once they've been domesticated. Where is your mother? Daddy said there would be four of you.'

'She went ahead with Milton,' said Mr Walters. Then his voice softened. 'I'm very sorry about your grandfather. He was a great friend. A dear man.'

'Yes, he was,' said Louella. She became quiet and for a moment her hostile manner vanished. Then her shoulders straightened and she recovered her composure. 'Please follow me.'

Even with the heavy suitcase and her small frame, Louella walked like someone twice her size, with large stompy steps that made the chandeliers shiver. Her short black hair was a mess, sticking out at the back as if she'd just woken up and hadn't bothered to comb it. She wore a loose cashmere cardigan that was far too big for her, grey trousers with yellow stripes, and black Chinese slippers with red plastic soles that slapped the marble floor.

'Daddy is in a meeting upstairs. He shouldn't be long.'

She took them into a draughty sitting room that was surprisingly shabby and dark. The chairs and sofa were the colour of roast chicken, with shiny, threadbare arms and backs and bits of stuffing popping out. The carpet was thin and full of holes. The drawn curtains sagged on their rails.

Thora fingered the projectionist's ring around her neck. The room had the same melancholy seediness as the Allbent Cinema in Grimli, with its dusty chairs and sticky floors. It would be a terrific place to set up the projector and watch films.

Louella put down the suitcase and folded her arms across her chest. From upstairs came the muffled sounds of an argument and the creaking of floorboards.

'What's the meeting about?' asked Thora, pointing at the ceiling.

'Croquet,' replied Louella, rolling her eyes.

'Crochet?' asked Thora.

'It's a game. A bunch of toffs in boaters bashing wooden balls through wire hoops. Ricardo's set up billboards all over London announcing the croquet palace he plans to build.'

'Hey, I *did* see something about that,' said Thora, snapping her fingers. 'I meant to tell you, Mr Walters.'

'Croquet is an aberration,' said Louella. 'Ricardo le Drone doesn't think so, however. If Daddy signs the document, the lawns of Snug will become a croquet players' paradise.'

'I'm sorry, Louella,' Mr Walters interrupted politely, 'but who is Ricardo? A croquet player?'

'A croquet *bore*. He's the millionaire Spaniard who wants to buy Snug,' Louella explained. 'He's upstairs right now, ramming croquet mallets down Daddy's throat!'

'That's horrific!' cried Thora. 'We must stop him!'

'Not *literally*,' said Louella. 'Anyway, the whole situation is very complicated. Grandpa's finances were already out of control when he first met Ricardo. He thought Ricardo really loved Snug and wanted to save it.'

'I know how your grandfather felt about croquet!' said Mr Walters. 'Out of loyalty, it's the one sport I would never dream of commentating on.'

'That's nice, but I'm afraid the vultures have moved in,' said Louella. 'Grandpa needed Ricardo's help. Now Ricardo is saying that on his deathbed, Grandpa gave him permission to go ahead and build croquet courts. But nobody else heard Grandpa say this.' Her eyes flickered. 'Except Blandina.'

'Who's that?' asked Thora. 'Your mother?'

'Step,' said Louella sharply.

Mr Walters was not surprised to hear of Lionel's financial problems. Hopeless, spendthrift, gallant old Len. He'd always known that Lionel struggled to manage his accounts, to keep the great behemoth that was Snug up and running. All Lionel had really wanted to do was pore over his Bathysphere and marine artefacts, not manage an estate. Mr Walters had not been to Snug for over a decade now and was shocked to find it in such a dilapidated state. The house and garden needed serious attention. He felt his eyes mist up. He could imagine quite clearly how susceptible Lionel would have been to this Ricardo fellow. Lionel would have done anything to save Snug. But croquet? Mr Walters seriously doubted it.

He shook his head. 'Croquet is a vicious game. I simply can't believe that your father would endorse this.'

'Ricardo calls croquet "the new snooker",' said Louella. 'He says the BBC and Channel Five are interested in televising croquet tournaments. First, because croquet brings out the worst in people, so there will be lots of depraved fights and squabbles. Second, it will be cheap as guts to film because you don't have to pay anybody. Just buy bushels of mallets and hoops, laser the lawns, paint the lines and haul in the wannabe celebrities. My stepmother is all for it.'

From overhead there came a CLANK, WHIRR, CLANK. The room began to shake. CLANK, CLANK, WHIRR, *SLAM!*

'Here's Daddy now!' said Louella.

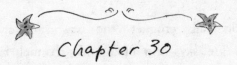

# Chapter 30

They all turned to see a large man with a youthful, rosy-cheeked face and incongruously white hair flying towards them in an electric wheelchair. He wore a velvet scarf, a green jumper and cheerful checked trousers.

Jerome Lancelot Bidet.

'By Jove! Mr Walters! How phenomenal to see you!'

'Excellent to see you too, dear boy.'

They embraced heartily.

'Thanks for all the postcards!' said Jerome. 'I've got a ten-year-high pile in my study!'

Mr Walters stood back to get a good look at his godson. Jerome's hair was whiter, his face rounder, his shoulders broader. It was still upsetting to see him in a wheelchair even though he had now used one for over a decade.

'I like your home, Mr Bidet,' said Thora. 'It's—'

'Jerome, please. Call me Jerome!'

'Righty-o, Jerome,' enthused Thora. 'Your abode has just the right amount of *squalor*. A bit of a relief after some of the places we've visited on our travels. One lady in Grimli – and I won't tar and feather her by name – covers her chairs with shrink-wrap!'

'Beastly,' said Jerome. 'Horrific. Frightful. Unthinkable.'

'I also like your wheelchair,' said Thora. 'Can you walk without it?'

'Not any more, dear girl. Polio got me in Western Baluchistan when I was on a lizard-catching expedition. Very bad luck given that they've eradicated polio in most places, at least in the Western world. I hope you are vaccinated, Thora. With all your world travelling, you never know what you're going collide with, do you? I must say, I do envy you lot.

Where have you come from most recently? And where is your champion swimmer? Are you hiding her from me? Does she still require a wheelchair, by the way? I've got a fleet in the raincoat room. Even a couple of electric ones. But I've gone back to manual. Keeps me trimmer. Did you know I've become a very serious gardener? It probably sounds ridiculous, the big explorer now trying to grow the world's biggest gooseberry, but I've found I enjoy it immensely. I did the avenue of limes myself. What do you think? Not original, I know. And all this ghastly business with your stolen boat. Do they have any leads? What did you say went missing – a sea-horse or something?'

Thora grew dizzy listening to him. But she liked him immediately. How different he was from Louella! 'A sea-unicorn,' she offered. 'Named Shirley.'

'Daddy,' broke in Louella, 'what's the decision?'

Jerome didn't look at Louella as he spoke. 'They'll start preparing the green tomorrow. Lasering in a week. The TV show starts filming a week after that.'

Mr Walters sighed as he sat down on the edge of the roast-chicken sofa.

Thora regarded him with concern. Though he had shown remarkable resilience over the past few days, her Guardian Angle was not well. Sleeping under wet newspapers in the rain and fog could not have helped! 'Mr Walters, you ought to go and have a rest.'

Jerome wheeled over to his godfather's side. 'Are you

all right? I want you to stay in the house, on the third floor. I'm worried about this flu of yours.'

'You've all got a lot on your plates,' Mr Walters said. 'This is not the best time for us to come here.'

Jerome took Mr Walters' liver-spotted hand and gave it a squeeze. 'I'm very glad you are here. All of you.' He sounded like he really meant it. 'Aren't we, Louella?'

Louella was slumped on a chair, in a posture that reminded Thora of a sulking Shirley.

'Louella? Where are your manners?'

When Louella looked up, there were tears running down her face. She muttered something then sprang up and ran out of the room. The glass beads on the chandelier clicked.

'Louella, come back!' Jerome's voice quavered. He smoothed his velvet scarf.

They sat in silence for a moment, listening to Louella's Chinese slippers retreating along the wooden floor. *Slap, slap, slap.*

At that moment, a thin, blonde woman with a sharp nose, unnaturally large, glossy lips and big gold earrings appeared in the doorway. At her shoulder was a dapper man with oiled black hair. He wore a mint-green seersucker suit and white shoes.

'Lovely to meet you all. I'm Blandina, Duchess of Snug. And this is Ricardo. Ricardo le Drone. Come with me and I'll show you to the folly where you'll be staying.'

Blandina's eyes lingered on Thora and widened. 'Is the girl all right? Why on earth is she wearing a *wetsuit*?'

'It's my Halla-Skin,' explained Thora. 'I always wear it.'

'If you'll excuse me …' said Jerome awkwardly, wheeling off, scarf flying. 'I'd better find Louella. She's had a lot to cope with lately. Please, Mr Walters, make yourself at home upstairs. Enjoy the four-poster bed. And Thora, you and your mother can help yourselves to supplies in the folly.'

Ricardo le Drone waited in the hallway, arms folded, white toe tapping, while Blandina ushered Thora out through the back garden to the folly and Cosmo followed behind. Mr Walters decided to tag along too.

Blandina's rubbery lips hardly moved as she apologised for the mess. 'Louella's grandfather never got around to sorting it all out and we haven't had time to clear the place.'

Then without coming inside, she glanced at her watch. 'Oops, I have to go!' she said, adding, 'I was in the middle of a meeting with Ricardo when you arrived.'

And off she went.

# chapter 31

Thora had always thought a folly was a spelling mistake and she was intrigued to learn that it could also be a garden house built to resemble a Greek temple. She had seen temples in Athens, but had not been allowed inside.

'Follies serve no other purpose,' Mr Walters said, 'but to impress, amaze and delight.'

'And provide shelter to itineraries,' said Thora, 'who'd otherwise be sleeping rough!'

Though Thora missed the *Loki*, she was always up for an adventure.

Set alongside a sparkly blue lake, the folly was as tall as a tidal wave, as white as the underbelly of a Chinese dolphin and about the same circumference as one of those award-winning giant California Redwood trees.

'Look,' said Mr Walters, pointing to three faint red chalk marks on the folly's sandstone base.

'Cricket stumps!' exclaimed Thora.

'I'd like to think I made those marks teaching Jerome cricket.'

Thora walked all the way around the folly and spied Halla's new home a few metres away.

'You go and see your mother,' said Mr Walters. 'I'm going back to the house to have a siesta.'

Cosmo went into the folly on his own, his tail dragging heavily behind him.

The grotto was an underground cave that looked a little like a half-submerged Swiss cheese.

'Helloo?' shouted Thora.

'Down here!'

Slippery steps led to a watery black floor. The grotto's walls were encrusted with oyster and abalone shells that seemed to wink back at Thora as she stared at them. She perched on a large shelf of stone and

peered through a porthole-like window at the lake and the little Doric temple on its opposite bank.

'It's got a lot more going for it than the Rock,' said Thora, remembering Halla's rather bleak home in Grimli. 'But it lacks a certain …'

'What it lacks in taste,' said Halla, 'it makes up for in cosiness. The Rock was very exposed. What I like about this place is the privacy.'

Thora laughed. 'And yet you've still got some company!'

Around a central basin of weathered plaster of Paris stood five nymphettes, and Neptune, clutching his trident and coughing algae-green water from a blowhole in his mouth.

Thora told her mother about everything she had just discovered in Snug House – about the croquet courts, the television show and the mystery millionaire, Ricardo. About Louella – her funny hair and grown-up voice and bossiness and tears.

Suddenly she stopped talking and ran her fingers through the water. 'I miss Shirley, though. I wonder what she's doing.' She gave her mother a wan smile. 'Do you think that she will be OK?'

'I'm afraid I can't make you feel better about Shirley,' Halla said softly. 'The laws of the sea are tough. We know that from our experience with your father. We just have to hope that she comes to no harm. Everything else is a bonus.'

# Chapter 32

Thora kissed her mother and returned to the folly.

First she passed through the anteroom with its empty hat stand and cardboard boxes stacked to form a neat tower. Then she entered the circular main room. It was rather messy, with two doors leading to what she presumed to be small sleeping quarters, and was dominated by a weird spherical structure unlike anything Thora had ever seen. It was made of metal and painted the colour of coffee yoghurt. On a bench were scattered maps, compasses, hydroscopes, a stack of books by a writer named William Beebe and masses of marine remnants. There were barometers, searchlights, telescopes, and an enormous light mounted on a gold-plated joint that looked as if it belonged on the top of a lighthouse.

On the walls was a selection of framed images: two men standing before another strange spherical object, the cover from a 1979 issue of *Dive* magazine showing a woman wearing an enormous scuba-diving suit, and the dust jackets of first editions of William Beebe's book *Half Mile Down* and Jacques Piccard's *Seven Miles Down*.

'I haven't had a chance to clear it all away,' came a voice.

Louella stomped into the folly carrying some empty boxes. Thora was pleased to see that she seemed herself again.

Louella stopped and looked around. 'Where is everybody?'

'They're all taking naps,' said Thora. 'It's been a long day.'

'For us too,' said Louella. 'It's taking ages to pack up my things.'

'They're yours?'

'They are now. Grandpa collected all of this stuff. It was his passion. He couldn't help himself. He was like a sort of gambler. If there was a Marine Collectors Anonymous, he should have been president. Nobody listened when I said his spending was getting out of control – until he bought the steel cable for the Bathysphere. Then it was too late.'

'Too late for what?'

'To recover the money. Spending is like gambling – it's an illness. I've read all about it. Anyway, he left me these things in his will. *All* of them. I'm the only one around here who's interested in aquatic subjects. Everyone hopes I'll grow out of it. Just like they hoped Grandpa would. Grandma was always trying to get him to donate everything to the National Maritime Museum in London. I'm thrilled he didn't, of course, but it is also a trial and a burden.'

'I'm interested in aquatic stuff too,' said Thora, thinking that Louella was a bit like Jerome after all. A shorter, more know-it-all version.

'Yes, of course,' said Louella. 'Living on a boat. I would like to interview you about that some time soon.'

'Interview me?'

'Excellent data-collecting procedure. One day I'll live on a boat. Anyway, I was going to keep all Grandpa's treasures in the folly while I created a database of his collection. I want to have it all listed and described so we know what we own.' She hesitated. 'Grandpa loved the bric-à-brac of the sea ... But I'm much more interested in the *living* sea, in ocean exploration. I want to be an aquanaut.' Louella knocked on the huge metal sphere with her knuckles. 'Some people wonder if this is an iron lung! Their ignorance never fails to astonish me!'

Thora leaned over and scratched her shin. 'What is it, anyway?'

Louella rolled her eyes. 'A *Bathysphere*, of course. An early method of ocean exploration. This one happens to be a genuine replica of Beebe's and Barton's 1930 model.'

'Does it work?'

'Not really. It's been mainly in storage. Like the original – which lived for a long time in a scrap yard at the New York Aquarium on Coney Island. When Grandpa heard that the original was getting spruced up for a big gala event, he was determined to try and get this one working again too. But he was just too unwell. So now I'm trying to restore it …' Louella took a deep breath. 'When it's up and running, it will be able to descend over 300 metres.'

'A mermaid can go even deeper,' said Thora.

'I'd like to meet one, then,' said Louella.

Thora bit her tongue and looked down. A small puddle had formed at her feet. How long were she and Halla going to be able to keep their mermaidness a secret? Mr Walters had said they should wait for just the right moment to reveal it.

'Do you want to go inside?' asked Louella. 'It's cramped and dark and it smells a little fusty, but it's very calming.'

'Maybe later,' replied Thora.

Louella shrugged.

'Most parts of the ocean go down about five kilometres. But there are trenches that can be up to eleven kilometres deep. That's 11,000 metres. The deepest trench of all is called the Challenger Deep, and it's located in the Marianas Trench. Only two people on earth have made it there: Don Walsh and Jacques Piccard, in 1960. Nobody has gone as deep since.' Louella pointed to the picture on the wall of a small woman dressed in diving gear. 'Sylvia Earle holds the record for the deepest female solo dive.'

'How deep did she go?' asked Thora.

'Three hundred and eighty metres, in 1979,' said Louella, 'before I was even born. But one day I would like to go much deeper. As deep as Walsh and Piccard. To the deepest part of the Marianas Trench!' Louella pointed to a photo on the wall.

Thora had never been that deep, but Halla told wonderful stories about the coral house she'd grown up in, her parents, the squid guards, the Sea Shrew. About the leopard sharks, sardines, chambered nautiluses, bioluminescent clouds of silver anchovies, about the sparkly little deep-sea fish that flickered bright blue lights, the blue-eyed wrasse that turned inside out and hid, the tiny sharks with glowing green eyes.

'The sea is the great unexplored mystery of the universe,' continued Louella. 'They send space shuttles and astronauts thousands of kilometres into orbit, devote millions of dollars to exploring outer space, yet only *one* woman has been 380 metres down.'

Louella looked very happy talking about the sea, almost like a different person, and for the first time Thora began to feel warmly towards her.

'Yes, the ocean remains the great unknown,' Louella went on. 'Yet it's in our own back yard.' She threw a handful of shells into her suitcase and looked out the window at the sparkling water. 'I'll tell you something, but you must not mention it to Daddy or Blandina.'

'What?'

'Grandpa took me down to the bottom of the lake a few months ago. After he bought the new cable. A depth of only six metres! Not much down there except a few old carp, weeds, mud and an ancient plimsoll. But the Bathysphere was leaking through the third porthole and we almost drowned. We didn't think it was fixable, but since we've got the Internet connected here, I've been researching alternatives. I've ordered a new set of valves and rubber tubes from a submersibles station in San Diego, and some special stuffing for the stuffing box.'

She pointed to a small funnel at the top of the Bathysphere.

'Also, I was going to paint it white, like the Beebe and Barton original, to attract sea creatures. Oh, and fix the propeller. It's a huge job. I was hoping to get it working in the lake this summer. You know, as a tribute to my grandfather.' She looked morose. 'But with all this croquet business, it will never happen. I'll have to satisfy myself with my scuba-diving lessons for now. And cataloguing Grandpa's things.'

'Hmm,' said Thora. Listening to Louella was giving her an idea. But she decided to keep it to herself for the moment. Louella suddenly looked like she could do with a bit of cheering up.

'You are definitely in need of a good ocean film,' Thora said, holding up the projectionist's ring.

'Ocean film?' asked Louella, brightening.

'And no need to move all this great stuff. Keep it here. We like it.'

'Seriously?'

Thora nodded. 'I have a distinguished feeling,' she said with a grin, 'that things are about to change around here.'

# Chapter 33

First, her ham radio had been cut off. Then the electricity. Finally, the landlord arrived at the door with two men in uniform and informed her that she had twenty-four hours to vacate the Saltworks Luxury Flats.

Pamela's eviction put her back in the Thames. She was forced to return to a mermaid diet of kelp, algae and sea foam, and the icy water soon gave her a streaming cold.

Thora, Mr Walters and the blonde had not returned to Chelsea Wharf. The woman on the *Stutch* had drawn her curtains when Pamela approached. From Miss Fishlock there had been no contact. Not a word. Even with her talent for self-delusion, Pamela knew that she had her work cut out for her if she was going to find them all in the great sprawling city that was London. Especially with the radius of her hunt confined to the water.

Pamela found a small hole under a nearby jetty and used it to stash her walking canes and some clothes, including her long rhubarb-coloured skirt with the built-in Bo-Peep hoop. She spent her days and nights swimming the Thames. For one half-hour each day, she surfaced, got dressed under the jetty, then begged passers-by on the wharf for food, or hunted among the rubbish bins for clues in old newspapers. It was not a nice way to live.

In the sea, the fish gave her a wide berth. Pamela didn't care. But she cared very much what humans thought about her. She hated the way children pointed and adult eyes flicked away. Their reactions bit deeply into her pride. It was certainly not the fate she had imagined for herself when she was an aspiring film star on the ocean floor. Not even when her film career fizzled in the World Above did she imagine it could come to this.

The green sea-unicorn was Pamela's only hope. She had to track it, catch it and deliver it to Mr Oto. But how?

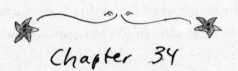

# Chapter 34

After a good night's sleep in the folly, Thora was back in the main house looking for something to eat. She was glad Mr Walters was not yet up. A lie-in would do him good. She hoped that Louella had enjoyed the film last night.

On the kitchen counter there was a note from Jerome:

**WE ARE OUT.**

Beside it sat a fresh loaf of bread with another note:

**HELP YOURSELF.**

In the cupboard, Thora found a rusty-looking toaster, which she took out and plugged into the wall. In its spotted reflection she fixed her ponytail. Then she put four pieces of bread into the toaster and pressed the lever down. Her tummy rumbled. She was hungry enough to eat a two-headed octopus!

On a shelf there were ten different kinds of

marmalade, six sorts of jam, two jellies, five tubs of honey and a jar of Marmite. As Thora was choosing between them, Louella stormed into the kitchen.

'How did you do that?' she demanded.

'Plug in the toaster? Like this—'

'No! The film! I tossed and turned all night trying to figure it out.'

'No need to lose sleep over it,' said Thora. 'Now, which jam do you recommend?'

'You're acting as if everything is *normal*. Well, let me inform you that it is *not*! Last night we were watching *The Poseidon Adventure* on the ceiling, for Christmas' sakes – on a projector that we didn't even plug in! It's not scientifically possible. I want you to explain how it works, step by step. I'm a quick learner. I pick up card tricks fast.'

'I'm not a magician. I told you all I know! And you forgot to tell me whether you liked the film – was it watery enough for you?'

'OK, if that's how you want to play it,' said Louella evenly, 'then *fine*. But consider it from my point of view. My father hasn't seen Mr Walters for years and then POOF, as soon as Grandpa dies, a phone call – *Hellooo, sorry, my boat's been stolen, MIND IF I MOVE IN? Oh, and by the way, I've acquired in my travels a girl in a wetsuit and her invisible mother!* Daddy's so gullible! How do we know who you are? You could be con artists! Gypsies! *Itinerants!*'

'That sounds like fun,' said Thora. 'But I'm afraid we're merely, well, *ourselves*.'

She had forgotten about the four slices of toast in the toaster, and they were now burning. She tried to pop them up, but the button was stuck. Smoke poured out and enveloped the kitchen curtains.

'Blandina's new curtains! We need blankets,' said Louella urgently. 'We need to smother it. Fire requires oxygen and if we deprive it of—'

'It's not fire! Just smoke.'

There was no time to worry about what Louella might think. Thora had to act fast. If she dampened the material, she could limit the damage. A fine trickle

quickly gained force and then a stream of water shot out of the top of her head and squelched the smoking curtains.

Louella looked incredulous. She handed Thora a tea towel. 'You'll have to clean that up yourself,' she said, coughing. 'We've had to let the daily go.'

'The daily what?'

'The *Portuguese* daily,' said Louella crossly.

'I didn't know you read Portuguese! Personally, I've always had trouble with that language. All those slushy Cs. When Mother swam the Tagus we stayed in an old converted castle covered in lichen. A little bit like your house, actually. Only more mosaics. And the toaster worked!'

'I'm talking about the *housekeeper*,' said Louella.

'Which housekeeper?' asked Thora, looking around.

Louella did not answer. It was as if the magnitude of what she had just seen was finally registering. She leaned against the counter, studying the smoky burnt curtains. Then from her vest pocket she produced a magnifying glass.

'That water came out of the top of your head,' she said. 'Didn't it?'

## Chapter 35

'Hey, not so fast!' Louella followed Thora out the door and into the garden. 'Let me inspect your head,' she demanded. 'I ought to warn you that my grandfather's magnifying glass never lies.'

'So the momentum of truth is upon us,' said Thora. 'Hold this, please.'

With a flourish like the one she'd seen a waiter in a Florentine restaurant perform as he served the fusilli, she slipped off her scrunchie and placed it in Louella's open hand. Then she shook out her hair and tilted her

head forward so that the shorter girl could see.

'It's a deformity,' Louella pronounced.

'It is *not* a deformity,' said Thora indignantly. 'It's a blowhole.'

'And you're a humpback whale,' said Louella.

'No,' said Thora, bracing herself for the revelation. 'I'm a mermaid.' She regarded Louella's sceptical face. 'Well, half. You see, my mother is a mermaid and my father a human.'

'What tosh,' said Louella. 'Mermaids are mirages. Even a simpleton knows that.'

'Mirages?' Thora refastened her ponytail. 'You mean like the sort of mirage that a thirsty traveller sees in the Sahara Desert?'

'Mirages can also occur when warm land air flows over the top of cool sea air. As light passes between the two temperatures it refracts—'

'Sounds like malarkey to me.'

'It's not malarkey. It's science.'

'Have you ever heard of a mirage getting married?' said Thora. 'Living in a boat? Raising a half-human child? Swimming the lakes of the world? Attending a banquet with the Queen of England? Do mirages make pineapple sea-foam birthday cakes and clean their rocks with pumice stones and make poultices out of seaweed for sick humans? Have you ever heard of that?'

'No, I haven't. I haven't because it is not possible.

Mirages are tricks of light.'

'My mother is not a trick of light.'

'You say that,' said Louella, 'but how would I know? I haven't seen her. Nor has Daddy. Or Blandina.' She adjusted her spectacles. 'It's well known that sightings of mermaids are really just sightings of common sea mammals – distorted by light, of course. Maybe this mother you call a "mermaid" is a mere sea cow. Or a seal. Or, more likely, maybe she's just like the rest of us and you are making this all up! Maybe she doesn't exist at all.'

Thora took Louella's hand and guided her to the grotto.

'Mo-ther! Are you there?'

There was no answer.

'Maybe she's gone for a swim,' said Thora.

'That would be convenient,' said Louella, hands on hips. She pulled out a black notebook from her cardigan pocket.

'Is that your journal?' asked Thora.

'It's not a journal,' said Louella. 'It's my logbook. For field notes.'

'Field notes,' said Thora. 'Sounds very – *au plein air*. The Impressionist painters worked out of doors – in meadows and poppy fields. I like to write in my journal when I'm outside, too.'

Louella clicked her pen impatiently. 'Let's say for a moment that your mother is, as you claim, a mermaid … and that you, ahem, are a half-mermaid, then you should have other mermaid features. It's one of Mendel's laws.'

'What are they?'

'Gregor Mendel, the father of modern genetics.'

'Who was the mother?'

Louella sighed. 'Haven't you learned *anything* at school?'

'I haven't gone to school. Well, I did go once, but it was not a very fortifying experience. The principal was a strange man who wanted me to unlearn what I know and learn it all over again – can you imagine? Mr Walters said I can learn much more travelling the world than sitting in a mouldy old classroom.'

'He said that?' Louella was impressed in spite of herself.

'Mr Walters is a man of the world,' said Thora proudly. 'Was this Mendel fellow one of those too?'

'No. Yes. He was a monk.'

'I met a lovely monk in northern Tibet. Do you know he never owned a pair of shoes? Now, that's the life.' And with two kicks, her windsurfing slippers flew into the air.

Louella continued. 'Mendel stated that human traits are passed down according to principles of heredity. Each germ cell contains a dominant and a recessive gene. He conducted his experiments with peas.'

Thora scratched her elbows. 'The pea man! Yes, we

visited his garden in Slovakia when my mother swam the Drina. I don't know how he made laws out of peas.'

'You saw Mendel's pea garden?' said Louella. 'You've been everywhere, it seems. I've only been to Brighton '

'Was it wonderful?'

'No, it was raining. I went there when I ran away from school. I wanted to see the sea, but I only got as far as the bus depot. I was expelled from boarding school for the rest of the term.' Louella looked at the puddle that had formed at Thora's feet. 'What's that?' she asked, making a face. 'Have you wet your wetsuit?'

'No! It's just another mermaid characteristic! My mother said humans can be strange about this. Don't worry, Louella. Mermaids tend to leak. And half-mermaids have scaly legs and purple feet. See?'

'That's just dry skin and poor circulation,' retorted Louella. 'Nothing that some moisturising cream and warm socks wouldn't cure.'

Frowning, she put her notebook back in her pocket and straightened her spectacles. 'This is getting silly. I've got to go. And I'm afraid I'm going to have to tell Blandina about the curtains. Otherwise I'll be blamed.'

'Just wait a few more minutes, Louella. I think when you see my mother—'

Louella was already walking back to the house. 'I don't think it's very nice of you to come here as a guest and behave in this fashion.'

# Chapter 36

Thora saw two burly men in blue uniforms walking across the great sloping lawn. One was carrying a surveyor's tripod, the other a large radio.

She swallowed hard.

'Louella, wait, please,' she called. 'If you had your own way, what would you like to see happen at Snug?'

'It doesn't matter what I think,' shouted Louella over her shoulder. 'It never has.'

'Let's make a hypotenuse and say that it did,' said Thora.

Louella gave her a half-smile. 'You mean hypothesis.' She stopped and turned around. 'OK. I'd like Grandpa back. I'd like Blandina to dematerialise.'

'And?'

Louella waved towards the water. 'I'd like to be able to take the Bathysphere down to the bottom of the lake. Maybe one day get it out to sea.'

'Anything else?'

'Pursue my ocean-exploration studies.'

'And?'

'Be the third person to go 11,000 metres down to the ocean floor.'

'Is that it?'

'Get Ricardo out of the picture.'

Thora gave her a long, watery look. She scratched her elbows, first one and then the other. 'What I don't understand,' she said slowly, 'is why you don't work with what you've got.'

'Meaning?'

'Stick to what you know. What you care about.'

'Water, you mean?'

'Yes,' said Thora. 'Let me see if I've got this right. You need to pay off your grandpa's debts so you can stay in Snug House.'

'Yes.'

'And you'll be allowed to stay if you let Ricardo build croquet courts and televise tournaments.'

'Yes.'

'What if you found another way to make money?'

'Like what?' said Louella sceptically.

'I was thinking that you could get the Bathysphere up and running, open a museum of marine artefacts, clean up the lake, throw in a few ecstatically acceptable water slides, and Bob's your uncle. It's so obvious! People would love it!'

'I've got no uncle named Bob,' Louella said rudely. 'And I think you meant aesthetically.'

'It was a figurine of speech,' said Thora.

Louella suddenly appeared weary. 'Blandina loathes the water. She won't even drink it.'

'But if your father liked the idea—'

'You don't understand anything. Daddy does what Blandina says. And Blandina always sides with Ricardo. It's like the whole place has been taken over by aliens wielding croquet mallets. And if it weren't croquet, it would be prize-winning gooseberries. It's a landlocked world round here.'

'It's not!' said Thora. 'Britain is an island!'

'People have no interest whatsoever in the ocean and even less in ocean exploration. Take all the silly aquaphobes at school – they think I am deeply weird. No one I know cares about what interests me. I accept that.'

'But *I* care!' objected Thora. 'And so does my mother. And Mr Walters.'

Louella took off her spectacles and polished them with the sleeve of her cardigan. 'With all due respect, Thora,' she said in her superior voice, 'you might have lived on a boat. Your mother might know how to open-water swim, or whatever it is she does—'

'Did.'

'And you might *think* you are half-mermaid.'

'Not think. Know,' said Thora.

Louella blinked. 'Even if you *are* what you say, it hardly qualifies you to lecture me about ocean exploration. Or to repair a Bathysphere. Or to act as a consultant to Ricardo le Drone, for that matter. Anyway, it looks like the decision has been made.' Louella waved towards the two men with their surveying instruments.

'It's not too late to change your father's mind,' replied Thora. 'Come with me.'

She shouted out to the men on the lawn. 'Did you two gentlemen get the message?'

'Which message?'

'The HOLD THE CROQUET PARK message.'

'No,' said one.

'What are you talking about?' said the other.

'What are you doing?' hissed Louella.

'There will be no lasering and levelling today,' said Thora firmly. 'You can put away your measuring tools for now.'

'Are you serious?' said the first man.

'I spoke to Ricardo this morning! Everything was go,' said the other.

'Well, this morning was a very long time ago,' said Thora. 'We're hoping to opt for the water park instead.'

'What water park?'

'The plans are still in the rude-documentary stage. But with your help, it will be upstanding! Louella here is the resident scholar, in charge of the Bathysphere, the museum of aquatic treasures and the database. I'll be Director of Fun and Games.'

'Are you an employee of Ricardo's?'

'She can't be,' said the other man. 'She's just a kid.'

'But tall for my age! And with some work to get done!' Thora replied. She removed the necklace with the projectionist's ring and held it up.

'You are getting very sleepy,' she said.

'You're a hypnotist, too?' asked Louella.

It was not the first time Thora had borrowed the technique of the world-famous hypnotist Boris the Remarkable. In Grimli, she had been able to persuade Holly's brothers, the lunkheads, that they were gorillas.

'I want you both to look at this ring. Your eyes are getting *heavy*.'

She spoke in a low, soothing voice and let the ring swing back and forth.

Four eyes followed.

Four eyes began to droop.

Four eyes closed.

'Now, when I clap my hands you will both think that you are … heavy construction workers! You'll deepen and dredge the lake. Clear it of weeds, but leave the carp and catfish alone. Now, please come with me.' She led the men to their truck and opened the door. 'Take a seat. I'll clap when I need you to start.'

'That ought to stall them for a while,' she whispered into Louella's ear. 'Now we just have to work out our plan. Then we'll speak to your father. After all, if you're lucky enough to have one, I reckon you ought to speak to him.'

'But we'll never convince Daddy to go ahead with it!' Louella objected.

'We will once he's seen the star attraction,' responded Thora. 'Seeing is believing. I'm sure my mother will be back from her swim by now. Come and meet her!'

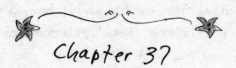

# Chapter 37

Miss Fishlock's career in fish had begun at London's first Aquarium Superstore on Plinkett Street, where she worked long, hard hours in the filtration department. One day a woman claiming to be a famous film star visited the shop. She wanted an aquarium. Only the best would do. She wanted a Belvedere Deluxe.

Miss Fishlock was alone in the shop. She explained that the purchase could not be delivered until the next day. 'In the meantime, can I interest you in a Superduper Sifter Silt Filter?'

'I don't use filters. I want your very best aquarium – now.'

Afraid that Pamela would change her mind, Miss Fishlock offered to deliver the aquarium herself. She loaded it into the back of her car, closed the store and drove Pamela home.

Pamela was delighted by Miss Fishlock's pink station wagon ('It reminds me of shrimp!'). She also seemed impressed by her driving skills ('You are so unruffled by this dreadful traffic!') and she exclaimed at her strength (Miss Fishlock carried the Belvedere aquarium unassisted into Pamela's penthouse flat). When Miss Fishlock noticed the ham radio on a shelf in the living room, and said that she had known how to operate one since childhood, Pamela clasped her hands together and, right then and there, offered Miss Fishlock a job. 'Come and be my driver! My assistant! My pair of legs – I mean my extra pair.'

Miss Fishlock had never felt so … well, appreciated. She thought she had nothing to lose.

But now she had lost everything.

Or so she felt as the *Loki* crashed into Albert Bridge and sent her down into the Thames. Sure that she was hurtling toward her own death, she made a vow to herself.

'IF I LIVE, I WILL CHANGE.'

For a few minutes it was so cold and dark under the water that it occurred to her that she was, in fact, dead. Never had she felt so alone, not even on Plinkett Street. She whimpered: 'I will use my two fat legs to serve anyone who helps me.' The wet pressed down on her. She couldn't breathe.

Then something nudged her from behind. She saw a green light. A swirl of silvery-green. She reached towards it. The light danced away, beckoning her to try again. Kicking out one leg, then another, she made her way over to a porthole, squeezed through and rose to the surface. A rush of air to her lungs made her cough and cough and cough. Then there was blackness all around.

Miss Fishlock had no idea how long she had spent lying on the river bank. But as she rolled over on to a bed of stinging nettles, and felt the pinch of the opera glasses on her shoulder, she knew beyond a doubt that she was very much alive and, furthermore, she had a promise to keep.

She felt something tickle her hand. The green sea-unicorn! The creature pulsed with the same extraordinary light she'd glimpsed in the water.

Miss Fishlock sat bolt upright. 'How can I ever repay you for saving my life?'

In the mud, Shirley used her horn to write:

### THORA.

'You want me to find your owner.'

Shirley nodded.

'Well, we'll go back to the Chelsea Wharf. I'm sure she'll be there, waiting for you.'

Shirley smiled and released what appeared to be a rainbow composed of small glittery diamonds.

It was the beginning of a beautiful partnership.

But for a while, it was a bumpy ride.

They had no transport. Miss Fishlock had left her

beloved station wagon in the Saltworks undercover parking lot and her keys inside Pamela's flat!

Also, Shirley required water. But her water jug had gone down with the *Loki*. Miss Fishlock had twisted her ankle in the crash and it took her forty minutes to locate an old plastic bag in a bin by the road's edge and fill it with water from the river – and well over an hour to walk back to Chelsea Wharf.

En route, Miss Fishlock told Shirley about Pamela's illicit trade in water creatures. Shirley was so distressed by this information that she released into the bag blobs the colour of the night around them.

It was almost midnight when they arrived at the wharf where the *Loki* had been moored and found nobody there. In her wet clothes Miss Fishlock was chilled to the bone. But there were more important matters to attend to.

Tenderly, Miss Fishlock lowered Shirley into the river, rinsed the plastic bag, polished the lenses of Pamela's opera glasses and scanned the harbour.

But it was Shirley who spotted what they were looking for. She used her horn and her snout to point.

The faraway but unmistakable glint of purple iridescence under the harbour lights.

Miss Fishlock squinted into the opera glasses and held her breath, waiting for the telltale flash of wet red hair. Yes, Pamela P. Poutine was in the river. Swimming. In their direction!

'This is our only chance,' Miss Fishlock said urgently. She hunched over and scooped Shirley out of the water. 'We must hurry. We'll take the bridge. I don't think she's spotted us!'

They crossed Battersea Bridge – Miss Fishlock limping on her bad ankle, Shirley sloshing around in her plastic bag. Using the duplicate key that Pamela kept hidden under the brick by the entrance, Miss Fishlock let them into the front lobby and then into Pamela's warm and rather humid penthouse suite.

She found her car keys immediately. Then from the kitchen she grabbed an entire box of freezer bags for Shirley.

It was not until they were leaving that Shirley noticed the aquarium. She swam agitated circles in her bag. Miss Fishlock carried her over to get a better look at the sea creatures – members of Shirley's own tribe.

The water was clouded and the animals looked miserable and hungry. A jewelled squid pressed its face and body against the glass and fixed the pair of them with a stare so forlorn that it made Miss Fishlock's eyes prick with tears. Shirley, however, was angry. Her neck straightened, her jaw was thrust forward, her nostrils flared, and she dashed her horn against the side of the bag.

'Let's free them,' said Miss Fishlock suddenly.

Shirley's nod was military-crisp.

EVENING STANDARD, 30 MAY

## UNDERWATER FIREWORKS IN THAMES

Residents of Chelsea Wharf and the surrounding area are still struggling to understand the source of a spectacular underwater light show.

Yesterday evening, at approximately 11 p.m. EST, a display of rainbow-coloured lights flared across the Thames.

Hundreds of people gathered at the river's edge to watch and take photographs. One witness described the colours as 'otherworldly like an aquatic aurora borealis'.

Marine biologist Gina Forx said that while scientists have not been able to agree on the cause of the light show, the phenomenon is most likely 'some sort of bioluminescence'.

Bioluminescence is the light produced by aquatic plants and animals - largely to attract prey.

*Tina Tennant*

EVENING STANDARD, 2 JUNE

## ESCAPE FROM LONDON AQUARIUM

Last night, hundreds of rare sea creatures and tropical fish were reported missing by the London Aquarium's director, Mr George Mastermann.

Security camera footage has revealed that a solitary thief broke into the aquarium at 2 a.m. Police suspect the thief to be a vigilante.

*Tina Tennant*

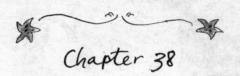

## Chapter 38

There was a splash and Halla swam into the grotto.
Her tail looked very shimmery in the darkish water.

'Mother, where have you been?' cried Thora. 'I want
you to meet a conspiring aquanut – Louella. Louella,
my mother, Halla.'

Not for the first time that day, Louella was at a loss
for words. She put her pen and notebook away. Her
cheeks flushed pink. Behind her spectacles her hazel
eyes danced. 'You're real,' she said eventually, in a
hushed voice – the sort of voice you might have
expected her to use in a library.

'First mermaid?' said Halla, her elbows resting lightly
on the edge of the pool. Her tail formed a graceful
purple question mark.

Louella nodded shyly.

Halla grinned. 'I've heard a lot about you. It's been
wonderful for Thora to make a new friend.'

'A friend?' said Louella, glancing at Thora.

'You don't have to look so shocked,' said Thora.

Louella flushed.

'A friend who is so smart!' added Halla.

'I've got a lot to learn,' said Louella modestly.

'Oh no, Louella. You're amazing! She's like a computer, Mother! I'll bet you're also good at geometry and algebra, aren't you?'

Louella's curiosity took over. 'Have you been to the deepest part of the sea? What's it like down there? Why aren't you there now?'

Halla did her best to answer Louella's questions.

Then Louella turned to Thora. 'How long can you stay underwater?'

'About forty minutes,' said Thora.

'Forty minutes!' replied Louella. There was no envy in her voice – just admiration.

'And how fast can you swim?'

'Standard dolphin speed.'

Louella did some calculations. 'That means you could swim back and forth across the Channel without surfacing in under an hour.'

Halla smiled. 'That sounds right.'

Louella shook her head in amazement.

'Thora,' said Halla, changing the subject. 'Didn't you have something to tell Louella?' While Louella studied Halla's tail, mother and daughter shared a few moments of hushed conversation.

'Righty-o,' said Thora, clearing her voice. 'To thank you and your family for your kindness in letting us stay here,' Thora said to Louella, 'Mother has offered to make appearances in the lake. People can descend in the Bathysphere and see her. A sort of adventure tourism trip, like they have up in Churchill, Manitoba, where groups get on a tundra buggy and go looking for polar bears. They don't know if they'll see one for sure … but not knowing is part of the fun!'

'As long as nobody takes photos,' said Halla firmly. 'Mother had enough of that on the long-distance swimming circuit.'

Louella chewed on a fingernail. She looked overwhelmed.

'It's only an idea. And I'd really like to help,' insisted Halla. 'Being myself is the only way I know how.'

They could hear voices approaching outside the grotto.

Thora sprang to her feet. 'Shark, who goes there?'

'It's Blandina!' cried Louella. 'And Daddy!'

'Perfect timing,' said Thora. 'I think we'd better get everybody together and make an announcement.'

'No!' Louella grabbed hold of Thora's ponytail to stop her rushing outside. 'What are we going to announce? That we have two hypnotised workers, a mermaid and a half-cooked plan for a water park?'

Thora smiled. 'Bingo!'

'We only have an idea. An idea is not a plan.'

Thora tapped herself on the head. 'It's all in here. Don't you want to go ahead?'

'I do,' said Louella briskly. 'But we're not ready for announcements. We need to put our own heads together first and decide exactly what we want. We've got to do this properly. By that, I mean methodically. Scientifically.'

'Why?'

'First of all, neither Daddy nor Blandina really likes the idea of water.'

'Why can't we use the gentle art of persuasion?' asked Thora.

'We can, but first we need to write it all down. Once we've defined our goals, we'll break it into smaller parts. Delegate.'

Thora put her hand on her hips. 'Who's that?'

'It means we need to decide who does what. A water park is a big idea and it will involve a lot of people.

We have to see what is realistic first.'

'Then we fire up the workers and it's a fate accomplished!' said Thora.

'No, it is not a *fait accompli*. When we've got our plan in writing, we'll make copies of it and hold a proper meeting. If we do our job well, Daddy and Blandina will agree. If not, we'll have to go to the next stage. Argument and persuasion.'

'Boy, this sounds like a lot of work!'

'Anything worth doing is a lot of work,' said Louella.

Halla made a splash with her tail in the water. 'Louella Bidet,' she said, smiling, 'I think Thora has a lot to learn from you about being human!'

# Chapter 39

Louella and Thora stayed up late into the night making their plans. In the back parking area, behind the house, the hypnotised workers sat dolefully in their truck, waiting for further directions. The girls took them tea and sponge cake, relieved that Ricardo had been called to London to sort out a business problem. Blandina had complained that the workers had not even begun to prepare the green. To calm her down, Jerome had taken his wife out for dinner.

In addition to their work supplies, Thora and Louella had brought with them two halogen torches, a basket of food that included a family pack of peanut M&Ms, and two puffy blankets. The tent on the back lawn was Thora's idea. 'I think best when I have access to fresh air through a tent flap,' she said.

'Oxygen is necessary for the human mind,' Louella agreed.

Louella had been powerfully affected by her meeting with Thora's mother. A mermaid was a miracle! That

made Thora half a miracle.

She placed a piece of paper in her grandfather's old manual typewriter and turned the knob. 'Now, we need a name for the water park. How about The Aquaculture Centre of Snug?'

'Not very poetical,' said Thora. She reached into their picnic basket and pulled out a banana. 'How about using your name? Bidet. The Bidet Water Park?'

Louella looked at her as if she was mad. '*Bidet* means "loo" in French.'

'You're kidding!' Thora laughed.

'No, I'm not. The *bidet* was invented in France in the seventeenth century. It's from a French word meaning "pony".'

'Isn't it amazing that something that sounds so pretty can mean something so—'

'It's a dreadful name. When I get older, I'm going to change my name to Rose. That's my mother's maiden name.'

'You didn't tell me your mother was a maiden! Does she grow silver bells and cockle shells and pretty—'

'You might have legs,' said Louella, 'but your knowledge of human language is very unpredictable.'

'Where is your mother?'

'In Oxford,' said Louella proudly.

'Mr Walters tried to make me get some Oxfords when I first learned how to walk. That was back when he didn't know much about raising half-human children. In the end, we decided windsurfing slippers were more practiceable.'

'My mother is Professor of Linguistics at Oxford University,' explained Louella.

'I adore that! We ate a lot of it in Sicily, smothered in garlicky red sauce. Yum.'

'Not linguini, you clot. *Linguistics!* The systematic study of language.'

'Oh. How come she doesn't live at Snug?'

Louella frowned. 'My parents are divorced.'

'What's that?'

'They don't live together. Most parents I know are divorced. I see my mother once a fortnight. But she's on a research study trip to Reykjavik at the moment.'

'We've been there. Mother swam the famous salmon river, the Langa.'

'Well, my mother's not swimming. She's studying the relationship between head circumference and language use in Icelandic speakers. She'll be back soon. Maybe you can meet her.'

'My parents must be divorced too,' said Thora, tucking the banana skin away.

'I don't think so,' said Louella.

'How do you know?'

'Grandpa told me that your father just disappeared.' Louella's voice softened. 'That's not the same as divorce.'

'Divorce would be better,' said Thora. She unfastened her ponytail and let her hair fall into her face. 'Then I'd get to see him. Like you get to see your mother.'

'I wish they weren't divorced,' said Louella. 'But they are, and there's nothing I can do about it. The hardest part is being polite to Blandina.'

'Why do you have to be polite to Blandina if you don't like her?' asked Thora.

'Because Daddy loves her.'

'I see,' said Thora.

'I was a baby when Mummy left. Grandpa and Grandma took care of me. They also hired a nurse for Daddy: a nurse from Essex named Blandina. He got polio just before I was born and was still getting used to life without the use of his legs. My mother didn't want to leave him in that state – or me, she says – but she found life here on the estate very difficult. She wanted to be a professor, you see, and if she had stayed here with us, she would never have been able to finish her PhD. Running the house and tending to her social duties would have taken up all her time. She didn't really understand the first thing about country houses. She grew up in London and her father worked at the children's zoo in Battersea Park.'

Louella reached out and placed her hand on Thora's shoulder. 'Maybe your father will come back one day.' Then she tapped the typewriter. 'Now, back to work. We have a lot to do before the meeting tomorrow.'

# Chapter 40

At noon the next day, a group met in the folly.

They sat at a longish card table that Louella and Thora had set up for the meeting amidst the barometers, compasses and maps, their chairs facing away from Lionel's Bathysphere.

The atmosphere was tense. Blandina had wanted Ricardo to attend the meeting, but he was not yet back from London and Louella refused to wait. Jerome had supported her.

Blandina arrived ten minutes late. 'What on earth is wrong with those workers? I spoke to them – quite harshly – but they just looked at me as if I wasn't there!'

Thora and Louella smiled at each other.

Blandina drummed her fingernails impatiently as Louella passed around copies of the Master Plan. Blandina had never liked the folly's moss-and-dank-lake smell. And the sight of all Lionel's odd treasures annoyed her. She wanted them sent to auction.

153

Plus, where was the girl's mother? Either she was very rude … or she did not exist!

Thora had alerted Halla about the proceedings. They had agreed she would wait in the grotto until the time came.

Louella had brushed her hair for the occasion and it curled prettily under her ears. But dressed in a starched white shirt and black trousers, she was all business. The plastic soles of her Chinese slippers slapped the stone floor as she readied herself for the meeting. When the last paper had been handed out, she cleared her throat. 'Thora and I have asked you here today to listen to our proposal. We would like you to consider an alternative to the croquet park. In your hands you have a copy of the Master Plan for Greenwater Park.'

The presentation lasted twenty minutes.

'Preposterous!' Blandina spluttered at the end.

'I don't want you to respond immediately,' said Louella. 'I will pour the tea and let you think about it.'

'Irish Breakfast,' said Thora apologetically. 'We're all out of Russian Caravan.'

'No, thank you,' said Blandina.

Louella ignored her. 'Thora and I will now step outside for a few minutes. We ask you to speak amongst yourselves. You can tell us your thoughts when we return.'

The girls left the folly and waited outside in the buttery midday sunshine.

'That was great!' said Thora. 'I'm sure they'll love it. How can they not? I reckon they'll give you a standing elation for that!'

But Louella was brooding. 'I think we've made a big mistake. We should have told them about Halla up front.'

When the girls re-entered the folly ten minutes later, Jerome looked depressed and Blandina's lips were turned down at the corners. Only Mr Walters made eye contact – a quick wink that was more an expression of sympathy than a congratulation.

Jerome broke the silence. 'Girls, it's not workable.'

Louella stood very still. 'Why not?'

'As Blandina points out, it's been done before. Water parks are nothing new. Slides, fountains, water skiing – I expect there are dozens of them around England. All the eco-friendly business is good, if a little trendy, and I quite like the museum idea—'

'Yes, a superb way to display Lionel's antiques,' said Mr Walters.

Blandina gave Jerome a nudge.

'But I just don't see this making the sort of money we need,' said Jerome. 'I'm very, very sorry. The answer is—'

'No!' Blandina smiled. 'It shows a lot of initiative and imagination, but, as Jerome says, it's not workable. It won't make money. Also, it's not fair on Ricardo. He's placed his trust in us. Now, gentlemen, girls, if you will excuse me.' She stood up and began to wheel Jerome towards the door.

'*Arrêtez-vous!*' shouted Thora.

'What now?' said Blandina.

'To recap,' said Louella, 'you liked the eco-friendly aspect. You liked the museum. But water parks have been done?'

Blandina pursed her lips, being careful not to smudge her lipstick. 'This is becoming ridiculous – all these watery games and childish fantasies. I've got a hundred things to do. We've given you a fair hearing, girls. But the croquet courts are going ahead. The workers were supposed to start yesterday. I'm fed up with these men loafing around in the trucks sipping tea. Come on, Jerome. You go and speak to them.'

'Wait,' said Louella. 'If your main objection is that "it's been done", then we'll show you now what makes our idea different from anything you or anyone else has ever seen!' She pointed to the Bathysphere. 'Do you know of a water park in England that takes people down to the bottom of a lake in a Bathysphere? *To see a mermaid?*'

'Louella, I think your father and I have been extremely patient,' said Blandina. 'Don't push it.'

'Blandina,' said Jerome, a faint warning tone in his voice.

Louella unbuttoned her cuffs and rolled up her sleeves. 'Don't you find it rather odd that you have not seen or met Halla?'

'What does that have to do with this?' said Blandina. 'With anything? You know what, Jerome? I've watched you indulge this daughter of yours, make excuses for her, apologise for her, and I'm afraid I'm sick to death of being Good Old Blandina who goes along with everything. Let's call a spade a spade. The girl is a spoiled brat and I'd like to see you put your foot down once and for all!'

Jerome regarded his second wife angrily. 'I *am* putting my foot down, Blandina.' He lifted his useless foot with both his hands and let it fall.

Mr Walters snorted with laughter.

Blandina, shocked by Jerome's outburst, fell silent. She stared at the wall above Louella's head as if trying to hold back tears.

Louella took hold of the wheelchair handles. 'I think it's about time we included Halla in our conversation.'

# chapter 41

Louella pushed her father out the door, down the grassy hill and over to the grotto. She felt strong and clear in her mind about her mission. Her father had stood up to Blandina! Louella had never thought she'd see it! Daddy had let Blandina boss him around for as long as Louella could remember. But he was too nice and too loyal to say anything back. In fact, Louella had started to wonder if he even noticed.

It was a relief to know that he *did* notice.

Thora jogged alongside the wheelchair. Mr Walters strode wheezily a few paces behind. And Blandina, in a confused tumult, stopped to remove her high heels and then tripped along some distance after them.

Louella crouched down and peered in through a window-like gap in the stones. 'Halla,' she said, 'my father is here to meet you. Could he come directly into the grotto?'

'Of course, if he doesn't mind getting a bit wet.'

Louella pushed the wheelchair as close to the small door as it could get and then Mr Walters and Thora joined to help lift Jerome on to the ledge that rose out of the water.

Halla was sitting on a rock beside Neptune. Her damp hair framed her face like a yellow wreath and her tail shimmered. 'Very good *finally* to meet you, Jerome. I hope you like the Greenwater Park plans as much as I do.'

Jerome fell silent. He took a deep breath but no words came. He stared – and then he spoke one word, which caught in his throat. *'Mermaid.'*

'Yes,' said Halla. She was used to having this effect on people and she gave Jerome time to recover himself.

Finally, the words began to loosen. 'This explains a lot,' he said. 'I see. I see.'

'I wanted to meet you earlier,' Halla began, 'but circumstances ...'

'Yes, circumstances,' said Jerome. Not even in his lizard-catching days had he been rendered so utterly speechless and charmed at the same time. And no lizard, not even the rarest Transcaspian Monitor, had humbled him so completely.

'Excuse me, Daddy!' said Louella, peeking in. She handed him her magnifying glass and disappeared.

'You are ...'

Halla smiled encouragingly.

'Perfect,' he whispered.

'Oh no, I am far from that, Jerome.'

'A ... fantastic creature!'

Embarrassed, Halla scratched her forehead.

'A real mermaid! I hope you don't mind my using this.' He waved the magnifying glass. 'I've handed it on to Louella but I used to use it on my field trips. I could always rely on it to tell me exactly what something was.'

'Not at all!' Halla reached out and touched Jerome's shoulder. 'I want to thank you for everything you've done for us. And also to congratulate you on your daughter. Louella is an extraordinary human being. Thora has learned a lot from her.'

Halla's words seemed to shake Jerome out of his

trance. He took her hand and and shook it vigorously. 'We've loved getting to know your daughter too! I am *so* sorry we didn't insist that Mr Walters effect this introduction sooner! We *were* starting to wonder a bit. And – let's be candid! – *worry*, too!'

A great banging noise on the grotto wall outside interrupted them.

'What is going on in there?' a voice shouted.

'Ah, that's my wife,' said Jerome. 'Blandina.'

Louella poked her head through the gap again. 'Daddy, I think Blandina wants to meet Halla,' she said.

Blandina pushed past Louella to peer into the grotto. Then she jumped back as if she'd been stung, her face blurred by incomprehension.

'*Oh my god, omygod, omygawd!* Is it real?'

From inside the grotto came a watery laugh. 'I could ask you the same question!'

'It speaks!' Blandina hissed.

'And it swims too,' came Halla's voice. 'I hear you're a bit of a hydrophobe.'

The word echoed like a schoolyard taunt – *hydrophobe, hydrophobe, hydrophobe* ...

'What on earth is it saying?' said Blandina. 'How does it know me?'

'*She,*' said Louella, 'not *it*. She. Thora's mother, Halla. She's a mermaid.'

Blandina turned in a circle. 'Is this some sort of trick? *Who are you people?*'

Mr Walters tipped his hat. 'I know it might come as a bit of a shock. Admittedly, I was a little unnerved when I first met Halla. But it's like anything a little out of the ordinary – you adjust. The human mind is terribly flexible. We can adjust to most things. Even that which at first appears impossible.'

'Or miraculous,' said Louella.

'Have you all gone mad?' said Blandina. 'Jerome?'

But Jerome was still examining, with a lizard expert's eye, the beautifully articulated scales on Halla's tail.

'Jerome!'

'Yes, darling?' Jerome said, without looking up. 'You know what? I think we ought to reconsider the girls' proposal.'

Blandina covered her ears with her hands. Then she turned and ran all the way to the house, without once looking back.

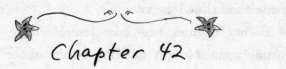

# Chapter 42

Upstairs in her bedroom, Blandina tried to pull herself together. She changed her clothes, ran a brush through her rather starchy blonde hair and stepped into a pair of black shoes with pointy toes and leather bows. In the small round mirror on the wall, she straightened her earrings, powdered her forehead and nose, and applied fresh lipstick.

With her long coffin-shaped purse under her arm, she marched downstairs into Jerome's office, opened the safe and located a file containing *Duke Lionel Bidet's Last Will and Testament*. Then she noticed the tiara and the child-sized calfskin suitcase. She'd seen these heirlooms before, but had never touched them. Now that she was alone and unobserved, Blandina tried on the tiara. It was small and bit into her scalp, but the weight of the gold and emeralds instantly made her feel like a born duchess. With growing confidence, she snapped open the suitcase to reveal an extensive collection of Penny Blacks, stamps collected by Jerome as a child. He had often referred to the great pleasure that this hobby had given him. Blandina flicked through the pages, marvelling at how something so boring could be so valuable. Then she smiled to herself and closed the safe.

Twenty minutes later, she found Jerome in the sitting room. He was speaking on the phone. There was a click and he twirled in his wheelchair to face his wife. He looked excited. 'I'm trying to get hold of Ricardo. I want to discuss the girls' idea with him. And with you, of course. Blandina, darling, I think the idea for a water park is inspired. And Halla will give it the special angle we need!'

'I don't think so,' said Blandina. Her feet were widely spaced. Her back straight. Her lips blood-red.

She reminded Jerome of a valkyrie, declaring war on a nation.

'Your father stated that he wanted Ricardo to build croquet courts,' Blandina said.

'Nonsense,' said Jerome with a laugh.

'It's right here,' said Blandina, brandishing the will like a mallet.

Jerome frowned. 'He only considered it in passing. I spent hours discussing alternatives with him. He had no intention of accepting Ricardo's proposal.'

'Perhaps you need to read the will more carefully, Jerome,' said Blandina.

'I read it before he died. I read it after he died.

Fine, I'll read it again.'

Jerome took the will and studied it. He removed the magnifying glasses from his pocket and lingered on the section that troubled him. He sat very still in his chair for what seemed a long time. Then he reached for the phone.

This was not the response Blandina had anticipated. 'Who are you calling?' she demanded, shifting on her kitten heels.

'My lawyer.'

The meeting was held twenty-four hours later at the lawyer's office in Snug village. Jerome, Blandina and Ricardo were present.

'I am afraid there is a serious problem here,' said the lawyer, lacing his white fingers together on the large oak table. 'There is a phrase, signed by Lionel, that reads:

> **I, LIONEL BIDET, GRANT RICARDO LE DRONE**
> **FULL PERMISSION TO CONSTRUCT AS MANY**
> **CROQUET COURTS AS HE CAN FIT ON TO THE**
> **GARDENS OF SNUG.'**

'Yes,' said Blandina impatiently. 'We know all that.'
'Because it is an amendment to an original claim, it was signed by the late Duke and dated.'

'Yes,' said Ricardo impatiently. 'We know all that.'

'The date reads 1 May,' said the lawyer.

'The day he died,' said Jerome, glumly.

'The time reads 2.10 p.m.'

'So?' said Ricardo. 'What's your point?'

'I have the death certificate here,' continued the lawyer, placing a piece of paper on the desk for all to see. 'Jerome, would you like to read out the time of your father's death?'

'11.22 a.m.,' said Jerome.

There was a confused silence.

The lawyer looked at each of them in turn and then said, 'If we are to believe these documents, then we would also have to accept that the late Duke amended his will after he died.'

'There must be a mistake,' said Blandina.

'Precisely my point, Blandina. There *is* a mistake. The doctor who attended the Duke swears that the time of death is accurate. Therefore, I can only assume that the will was amended after death. Clearly, not by the Duke. But by someone hoping to profit from the Duke's death.'

'Late again,' said Jerome.

'This is libel,' objected Ricardo.

'It is illegal to alter another man's will, Mr le Drone, be he alive or dead. I have consulted a handwriting expert who will be happy to testify that this amendment is a forgery. We can take the matter to court. Or we can pretend it never happened.'

Ricardo looked to Blandina. She did not catch his eye.

Blandina left Snug with her suitcases that night. Ricardo le Drone was never heard from again.

## LIPSTICK VIGILANTE STRIKES AGAIN

Bristol police are investigating a break-in at the Bristol Zoo Aquarium last night that resulted in the disappearance of dozens of valuable sea creatures, including a rare spotted dragon sea-horse.

There were no witnesses to the incident, which is believed to be linked to similar incidents in the Greater London area last week.

Written in lipstick on the glass of the aquarium were the words *Gone home*. Police are looking for a lone suspect, possibly a woman, with environmental concerns.

Black-market trading has not been ruled out.

*Tina Tennant*

EVENING STANDARD, 10 JUNE

## EMPTY TANKS

Oxford police are scratching their heads over the mystery aquatic vigilante who has freed the sea creatures from the prize tank at the Oxford University Museum of Natural History. Linking the incident to the Bristol break-in three nights ago is the message written on the tank in red lipstick: *We're never coming back*.

Footage from security cameras has revealed that the vigilante may not be acting alone, as had been assumed, but may have a very small accomplice. Police are not at liberty to reveal more.

Environmental groups across England met in London last night to discuss the implications of aquatic vigilantism.

*Tina Tennant*

## chapter 43

Pamela was caught between a wharf and a cold river. If she hid in the Thames, she had to keep finding a new place to store her canes and clothes. If she slept rough on land, she risked arrest. As occurred that very evening.

'She's a feisty one,' said one policeman to his mate as they dragged Pamela along the wharf. She'd thought she could get away with just one night on the docks, but she was wrong.

'Come on, Pam.'

'You know her?'

'Oh, yes. Pamela and I have met before, haven't we, Pamela? I was hoping you would have an honest job by now.

'Not still smuggling precious sea creatures out of London, are you? There've been some new laws introduced – anyone now caught hunting contraband ocean creatures will be treated like a proper criminal.

About time!'

'I *demand* a lawyer! How *dare* you treat a minority in this fashion! I'll sue you! I've done nothing wrong!'

'Everyone is a minority these days, Pammy.' The policemen handcuffed her and climbed into the front of the car. 'Read the sign: NO ITINERANTS OR SLEEPING ROUGH.'

They drove to the station and carried her into a crowded cell.

'Only one night in the slammer this time,' the first policeman said. 'But I don't want to see you in here again – for sleeping rough or for any other hanky-panky!'

The Folly
SnuG Estate
SnuG-shire
A melon and cauliflower
sort of June day
11 o'clock AY. EM.

So. Lovella got what she wished for.
Blandina has dematerialised.
yesterday we waved her goodbye (from driveway).
We were all a little sad. Farewells are hard.
Like the last page. No — like reading the last
LINE of a book. (you don't even have to LIKE
the book, to feel a funny pang as you close it.)

But also — I've noticed that humans are often
of mixed minds and not always happy when
they get what they wished for. (Lovella
DID NOT WANT A PARTY TO CELEBRATE Blandina's
DEPORTATION (SHE even DECLENSIONED my
OFFER TO BAKE AN Angel Cake). she
said that no matter HOW delicious the
CAKE might be... It WOULD TASTE Bitter.

Then Lovella reported more
extravagantly bitter news early This morning

Blandina HAS STOLEN THE
PRICELESS EMERALD TIARA
THAT BELONGED TO THE DECEASED
DUCHESS — LIONEL'S WIFE & IMOGEN'S
BEST FRIEND ON EARTH. IT WAS SUPPOSED
TO BE HANDED DOWN TO Lovella...
(Lovella says she wouldn't be
caught DEAD in a tiara — but it is
the principality that counts.)

Possibly WORSE — Blandina has also
taken Jerome's childhood stamp collection!
From what I can hunt & gather, this
stamp collection is extremely precious
to HIM (Like my journal to me).

Unlike my journal — which is of
sentimentality value — His stamp collection
is WORTH a lot of money (like Shirley)
dear
— it contains hundreds of R A R e
stamps including a sheet of the first
Postage stamps used in Britain — in MINT
SMELLING CONDITION (important for)
Stamps.

Even the suitcase that
held the collection is an
example of an early victoriana antique.

Mr Waters says that the
theft is of a *low* order and
that Blandina is a ScoondRella.

Louella said that from now until
the end of time, T_HAT_ WOMAN shall
be referenced as BLANDINA—non—
GRATA. (Even so... Jerome seems a
little mournful.)

But all is not a field and Valley
of tears. (Actually — there is no time
for marooning because ....)

GREEN WATER PARK IS
GOING AHEAD!

Everyone is STATIC to get started.

The GREEN part is a small
tributary to dear Shirley. Also, it
just so happens that GREEN
is BOTH my & Lovella's favourite
colour for all times.

As I write this, I can hear
the WHIRR of the digging machines
as the workers DREDGE the lake.

Lovella is organising the museum
and Mother is planning her
swimming routes. She can't wait until
the lake is re-filled. (In the meantime,
she is feeding kelp soup to Mr Walters.

He seems to need a lot of
sleep all over again. But on
the ⊕ side of things, he
has almost finished an entire
jar of gentleman's relish (ordered
by Jerome from Fortnum's as a special
treat.)

# Chapter 44

Of course, it didn't happen overnight.

There were headaches, arguments, one or two disasters (the first set of valves were too small and the Bathysphere leaked on a trial run).

And everyone had their role to play – especially the two surveyors, who dredged the lake in record time. They performed all the large building tasks, freeing up everyone else to get on with the rest.

Halla prettied up the banks of the lake by scrubbing the rocks with her pumice stone, washing the windows of the folly and braiding water ferns, bulrushes and lily stalks. She also supervised a specialist hired to scale the grotto and bring the polish back to Neptune and his flock of nymphettes.

Jerome and Mr Walters (when he felt up to it) busied themselves with the important tasks of fixing wheelchair ramps, repairing broken stairs and windows and spreading the news of the impending water park to the media.

The Lionel D. Bidet Maritime Museum for Marine Curios was established. The database would require more work, but then again, databases were, in Louella's words, 'a lifetime commitment'.

Louella was busy preparing the mini-lectures that she would offer on ocean exploration and all aspects of aquaculture from temperate to tropical.

The boats were purchased. And the fun park erected.

The fun park had been Thora's idea and served, she announced, 'no other purpose but to impress, amaze and delight!' It consisted of two giant water slides, five fountains, a water-pistol range, and a swimming area for snorkelling, surfing and scuba diving.

Mr Walters was a little worried about the swimming area. 'Every English person dreams of fun in the sun,' he said, turning up his collar and pointing at the rain-drenched sky, 'but very few English people get to experience it!'

So Jerome sacrificed one of his vast Paxton-style greenhouses. It was cleared and transported to the edge of the lake, where, straddling the grass and water, it acted as a sort of sun-conductor for water sports.

The films, Thora decided, would be shown in the sitting room with the roast-chicken sofa. The atmosphere was perfect: comfortably shabby yet stylishly ornate. When the lights were dimmed and the high-ceilinged room welled with shadows, Thora was taken right back to her grandmother's cinema, the Allbent, in Grimli-By-The-Sea.

Finally, the stuffing, valves and rubber tubes arrived from San Diego. A submersibles expert was hired to install them and to perform a maintenance check on the Bathysphere. Fully restored, it could now take people, two at a time, to the bottom of the lake where they might – or might not – see a mermaid. At Halla's insistence, Louella and Thora painted several signs:

## NO CAMERAS ALLOWED.

Thanks to everyone's hard work (especially the hypnotised surveyors), Greenwater Park was ready for the public by 30 June.

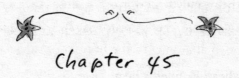

# Chapter 45

The warmer weather made pedestrians generous. One man gave Pamela five pounds and a newspaper. She bought some ghost crabs in batter and a fizzy lemonade drink and sat down in a spot of sun on the Chelsea Embankment to eat. Though pleasant, there was a chilly burr on the breeze, and when she'd finished her snack, she pulled the paper up over her like a blanket.

Clues often come at unexpected times.

In the gossip column 'The Londoner's Diary', right there in her lap, was the headline:

DUKE OF SNUG'S DAUGHTER AND FRIEND THORA
GREENBERG PROVIDE WATERY GREEN ALTERNATIVE.

Pamela's heart skipped a beat. *Thora?*

She read on:

Last month, the controversial firebrand Ricardo le Drone cancelled his plans to build five Olympic-sized croquet courts on the late Duke of Snug's ailing estate.

Days before signing the deal with the BBC and Channel Five, the late Duke's grand-daughter, Miss Louella Bidet, eleven, only child of the new Duke, Jerome Bidet, and her friend, Miss Thora Greenberg, ten and three-quarters, trumped the flamboyant millionaire croquet aficionado Ricardo le Drone with their dazzling aquatic alternative.

The two girls assured nay-sayers that the park would open at the end of June. They have kept their promise. Snug House now boasts a Maritime Museum and aqua-educational centre; a children's water park with slides and spray fountains; and a sitting-room cinema specialising in old sea films. But about the *pièce de résistance* the girls were mysterious. 'Seeing is believing!' they said.

Greenwater Park is now open to the public.

(What we'd like to know is where did they get their workers? We didn't think it was possible in England to complete a construction job so quickly!)

*Tina Tennant*

So the gimlet girl was in Snugshire! How extraordinary! How wonderful! How easy!

Pamela laughed aloud. The breeze softened and the sun popped out from behind a puffy white cloud overhead.

Finally, the pieces were falling into place.

She reviewed the facts.

First, the crash.

Then the kerfuffles: the disappearance of Miss Fishlock, Shirley and the family.

There was only one way to explain Miss Fishlock's disappearance: Shirley had escaped and Miss Fishlock was too scared to face Pamela empty-handed.

Pamela examined the scar on her palm where the little green sea-unicorn had lanced her. Then she massaged her neck, closed her eyes and tilted her face to the sun.

Shirley would have returned to the wharf. She was a good swimmer and, as Pamela had experienced first-hand, well able to defend herself.

The family had then simply left London to visit

friends in the country. Probably contacts of that old geezer grandfather. Pamela recalled his posh accent and deep baritone voice. People with voices like that *always* had friends with estates in the country.

It was all so deliciously simple!

Knowing their location did not exactly restore Pamela's shimmer, but sitting there in the sunshine, she could feel the kick returning to her tail. She had a location. Now she had to find a lift to Greenwater Park so she could get her hands on that *'pièce de résistance'*, sell her to Mr Oto and start her new life.

She looked down at the newspaper. Her eyes fell on the name Tina Tennant.

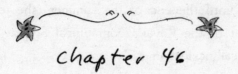

## chapter 46

In one week, announced the Snug village newsletter, Greenwater Park had shattered all previous water-park attendance records.

Resting in his bedroom on the third floor, Mr Walters took stock.

Thousands of people had already taken advantage of the warm weather to make the journey to Snug – to play in the water park, watch old sea films and try to glimpse a mermaid in the Bathysphere. The queues for the Bathysphere often extended a kilometre or two.

Snorkelling in the lake became increasingly popular when it was decided that customers should be allowed to bring their own equipment. Four lifeguards and water-safety instructors with scuba and snorkelling qualifications were hired to provide lessons and inspect equipment.

One of the surprises in the mix had been Louella, who discovered that she had an unusual gift for public speaking and teaching. After her inaugural lecture to her science master and classmates about ocean exploration in the late nineteenth century, she had been bombarded with calls from science instructors and science organisations around the country. 'I'm fully booked until the end of the summer,' she told the president of the Royal Geographical Society. 'You'll have to call next summer.'

Jerome had been forced to abandon his project to grow the world's biggest gooseberry in order to assist with the catering, as visitors were starving after a day at Snug. He used only certified organic suppliers and evolved a simple but wholesome and delicious menu of soups, salads, pastas, breads, juices and cakes. Thora encouraged him to turn his green thumb to planting and growing the fruits and vegetables his dishes required. Soon the garden in his extra greenhouse was pulsing with life, as the first green tips and shoots of organic carrots, peas and beans peeped through the rich black soil. Jerome was delighted to be applying his considerable botanical skills to something practical – and thrilled that customers were raving about his carrot and gooseberry soup.

Life certainly had changed since his lizard-catching days in faraway places!

Milton managed the water-park staff and gave daily sailing lessons himself on his catamaran. Mr Walters recommended ginger tablets to help aid seasickness and they proved so effective that Milton placed a down-payment on a five-metre speedboat. He also cancelled his appointment with the doctor to remove his tattoo.

And Thora involved herself in everything. She and Louella took turns descending with the 'noble public', as Louella called them, to the bottom of the lake in the now-functioning Bathysphere. To Mr Walters' great sadness, one BBC journalist was sent away in disgrace after a digital camera was found hidden in her handbag. Another had to be hauled to the surface when he attempted to videotape the waving mermaid on his camcorder.

People who managed to glimpse Halla were often overwhelmed. Or awed. Their world was expanded. They left Snug Lake feeling that if Halla was possible, what else was down there? Louella liked to reinforce in her lectures on the life and death of phytoplankton that only a tiny fraction of the ocean floor had been explored; only a fraction of the world's sea creatures studied.

'In this single tiny drop of sea water exist thousands of unknown, unidentified microbes and viruses – life forms that are crucial to the existence of planet water. One-celled marine plants such as coccolithophores are the foundation of the marine food chain and can influence the Earth's climate!'

As for Halla – well, she simply enjoyed herself, swimming daily in the lake, appearing when and if she

felt like it to wave or smile at the Bathysphere or the
snorkellers. Sometimes she swam up quite close. Once
she even blew a kiss to a very old man, who was so
overwhelmed by the experience that he developed
palpitations and had to end his adventure abruptly.

# Chapter 47

Pamela installed herself at Chelsea Wharf near where the *Loki* had been moored, and waited.

The journalist, Tina Tennant, appeared on the fourth day. A petite, pretty young woman with long shiny black hair parted down the middle. Lightweight leather jacket. Knee-length boots with rubber heels. A big square bag dangling from her shoulder. She lingered. Made a call on her mobile phone.

When Tina had finished her call, Pamela took a deep breath and pulled herself up on to the wharf. Hair flying, skirt dripping, she smiled winningly. 'Are you looking for me, by any chance?'

The girl looked surprised. 'Halla? I thought you were blonde!'

'And I thought you would be here four days ago,' said Pamela peevishly.

'I'm sorry, I was in Bristol. Then I had to go to Oxford. Anyway, I'm here now. You said – what was it?' she checked her notebook. 'That I "would learn something to my advantage about the so-called open water swimmer".' She looked up 'Why "so-called"?'

'Do you have a car?'

'Yes, I do. Why?'

Pamela shook the seaweed from her walking canes and placed them in front of her. She grasped the handles and lurched towards the girl.

Alarmed, the journalist put away her mobile phone. 'Do you need some help?'

'I'm Pamela P. Poutine,' Pamela said, holding out her hand. 'And Halla, the so-called world champion open-water swimmer, is a mermaid.'

Less than an hour later, the mermaid and the journalist were in Tina's company car, heading for Snugshire. Pamela tucked her tail under the seat and fluffed out her ragged skirt.

Tina took a deep breath and leaned back in the driver's seat. 'So let me get this straight,' she said. 'Halla must be the mermaid at Snug.'

'What mermaid at Snug?' said Pamela.

'*What mermaid?* Where have you been?' responded Tina. 'You must be the only person in England who hasn't heard about her.'

Pamela had assumed that the *'pièce de résistance'* was Shirley, but with a glugging heart she realised she'd been wrong. It was Halla.

'The traffic on the M25 is exceptionally heavy. Expect long delays, especially as you approach the Snug House turn-off at the A203. The combination of unusually hot days and the popularity of the Duke of Snug's new water park seems to be the cause. Drive safely and stay cool. This is Mandy Rood with your local traffic news. Over to you, Brian, with a story about the mysterious Lipstick Vigilantes. Looks like they've struck again. Where this time, Brian?'

Pamela impatiently switched off the radio and pretended to cross her legs.

'Hey,' said Tina, switching the radio back on, 'that's the story I'm covering. Well, *supposed* to be covering. My boss will be furious when he finds out what I'm doing now.' She turned the volume up high then switched the radio off again. 'Oh, Christmas! We missed it.'

Pamela did not enjoy the first leg of the drive. The journalist plied her with questions. How did she know that Halla – the open-water swimmer – was a mermaid? Did anyone else know? How did Pamela fit into all this? Could Pamela arrange an interview?

The mermaid at Snug was not talking to the press. Nevertheless, Tina could not suppress her excitement. Nobody had ever knowingly interviewed a mermaid before, but with Pamela's help, this could be her break. It would get her off the wretched water circuit. If she played her cards right, it would change her life. She must sell syndication rights immediately!

On the more personal questions, Pamela grew evasive. She was starting to wonder how she was going to get rid of Tina once they arrived at the Bidet estate. Halla would never agree to an interview.

Tina pulled into a petrol station to refuel. 'I'll get a few sandwiches. Any preferences?'

'Egg salad,' said Pamela, momentarily forgetting her troubles. She was famished. 'And a bottle of soda water and a few newspapers.' Mermaids of a certain age had less than two hours before their tails began to dry out.

While she waited for Tina to return, Pamela caught sight of her face in the window of a neighbouring car.

Tummy clenched, she flipped down the passenger's

sun visor to take a closer look in the mirror.

Weeks of living as an itinerant mermaid had taken their toll. She was appalled to see that her iron-grey roots had taken over – her hair was hardly red at all! Her complexion was ruddy from weeks spent out of doors. Her eyes were ringed with dark circles. Her chin sprouted two whiskers!

She looked down, imagining herself through Tina's eyes.

Her rhubarb-coloured skirt was filthy and torn, the Bo-Peep wires sticking out like antennae. Her nails were black at the ends of chapped fingers.

There was a knock at the window. Pamela wound it down.

'Egg salad, newspapers and soda,' chirped Tina, spilling her purchases into Pamela's lap.

The presence of the tiny, tidy, sweetly scented little journalist girl in the driver's seat beside her didn't exactly help. Even her name was dainty and feminine. Tina Tennant. And her posh accent made Pamela feel like a great lumbering creature of the deep.

'I need a makeover,' Pamela said urgently. 'An *extreme* makeover. Any ideas?'

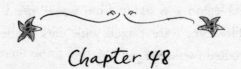

## Chapter 48

The traffic lightened once they passed the turn-off to Greenwater Park and they were soon in the village of Snug. Tina parked the car on the high street and she and Pamela headed towards the Bib & Tucker, where a large sign in the window read:

### CLEARANCE SALE. EVERYTHING MUST GO!

The store was packed with aggressive, sharp-elbowed women plundering the racks and sales tables.

'You go ahead,' said Tina. She looked very out of place in the shop. Her clothes were a little too expensive, her figure a little too trim. But she had offered to pay for Pamela's makeover. With what she could get for world rights to her story, she would be able to buy a Caribbean island, or maybe two! 'You help me, and I'll help you,' she'd said, producing a shiny credit card from a stylish orange leather wallet.

Pamela took a deep breath and plunged in. As she flipped through the dresses, she could hear Tina arguing in a low voice into her mobile phone. 'No, no. I have a *much* bigger story. No, I have not "lost" it. Listen, I'll get back to you, OK? I'll get on to the vigilantes later.'

Pamela felt excited to be out on the town. 'Tina!' she boomed. 'Could you help me? I need a size 18 in that cranberry skirt. I'll try a size 20, too. Bring them to the change room. I'm going to try this on.' She held up a scarlet dress. 'And if you see some tops that would look lovely … maybe a light-coloured blouse would do the trick.'

Everyone stared. Tina looked mortified as she threaded her way through the aisles gathering clothes.

She could not bear the idea of a half-dressed Pamela and her eyes were closed as she thrust the clothes through the gap in the dressing-room curtain.

'It's fun, just us girls, isn't it?' cooed Pamela.

After what seemed like hours, Pamela settled on a tomato-coloured rayon skirt in size 18, a loose white peasant blouse – 'perfect for the heat' – a large purple handbag and a rather shiny straw hat with a wide brim and pink felt bow. 'You can't be seen in the country without a hat, my dear.' Pamela had read endlessly about the country set in *Tatler*, *Hello* and *English Country Living*.

'Is that right?' said Tina, signing her name on the sales slip. Tina had grown up on a vast estate in Dorset and was no stranger to the country set.

Next they went to the hairdresser's, Odette's, where Pamela opted for the Colour & Cut Special With Free Manicure. Tina waited impatiently by the door, flipping through fashion magazines, as Pamela lurched from sink to chair to hairdryer.

A large-bottomed woman in stretchy nylon pedal pushers did Pamela's nails while she sat under the dryer. 'Same colour for the toes?' she asked, waving the bottle of beige nail polish.

'Won't be necessary.'

'Let me have a look, luv. Toenails are the great forgotten female detail.'

From the other side of the room, Tina flashed her

credit card. 'Go on, Pamela. Splash out!' The idea of selling world rights had made her expansive.

'No. But I'll buy a pair of those wonderful toenail clippers.'

'You must watch those. They're sharp as shark's teeth!'

Precisely, thought Pamela. They would be useful if that wretched little sea-unicorn tried to bite her again.

Pamela tucked the clippers into her new bag. She was delighted with her hair colour and wrote down the number and brand on a small card for future reference.

The transformation was remarkable. Back in the car, Pamela could not help peeking at herself in the sun-visor mirror.

Tina switched on the radio. 'Strangers in the Night' swirled through the car.

'Frankie!' cried Pamela.

'Frankie who?'

'Oh, you stupid girl! Turn it up!'

# Chapter 49

They drove through the stone gates of the Snug estate and travelled down the avenue of limes, passing two large wooden signs for Greenwater Park marked with arrows. Ignoring a sign that said PRIVATE, Tina drew up near the front staircase of the great custard-coloured mansion.

The door burst open and a man in chequered trousers flew down the ramp in his wheelchair. The pigeons scattered. 'Can I help you?'

Pamela had rehearsed her lines. 'I'm here to see my dear friends Thora and Halla,' she said. 'It's a surprise.'

Jerome gave her a puzzled but not unfriendly smile. 'And you are?'

'Pamela. Pamela P. Poutine. Actor. Quite famous, actually.'

'Blimey!' beamed Jerome. 'What have I seen you in?'

'Oh, don't worry about it,' said Pamela. 'I specialised in aquatic films. You're probably too young to remember.'

'Pamela P. Poutine,' he said slowly. He looked at her.

Pamela shifted nervously. 'I've got it!' he said, clapping his hands.

'Got what?'

*'With these lips I fill your lungs with air, your heart with love.* It was you who gave mouth-to-mouth resuscitation to Neptune!'

Pamela stood speechless.

'I saw you every night for six months. The Niger desert. The only cinema. What was the film called? *Neptune's Mother-in-Law?'*

'No,' Pamela corrected, *'Neptune's Stepsister*. I didn't think they'd released that film.'

'And you were wearing that *amazing* tail! Wonderful what cinema can do! It's why I bought the statue of Neptune for our little grotto! A sort of tribute to the King of the Sea! Well, come on in! Halla and Thora are both working right now, but they'll come over when the water park closes. I'll tell them you're here!'

'That would be lovely,' said Pamela with a flutter of her lashes. 'So they're all here – Halla, Thora and *Shirley*?'

'Absolutely. Miss ... Mrs ... Poutine ...'

'Call me Pam.'

'Smashing, Pam. And your friend?'

Pamela glanced over her shoulder. Tina was hunched over in her car seat, talking on her mobile phone. 'Oh, her. She's not my friend. She just drove me. If you'll excuse me a moment ...'

Pamela lurched back to the car and whispered, 'You can go now.' Despite her tiny size, Tina Tennant was suddenly a very large inconvenience.

'Go? But what about Halla? My interview?'

'There will be no interview,' said Pamela coldly. 'Halla isn't even here, as it turns out.'

'I don't believe you!'

'Thank you for the drive. Now go, or I'll have the Duke call the police and charge you with harassment.'

Tina stared, dumbfounded. Then her jaw was thrust forward and her eyes narrowed. 'You lied.'

Pamela turned and moved away.

Tina rolled down the window. 'How dare you treat me like this! After all I've done for you!'

Pamela waved goodbye, but it was more the gesture one uses to shoo away an unwanted sea louse.

It had been a long time since Pamela had enjoyed the sort of audience that Jerome Lancelot Bidet offered up with tea and lemon-cream biscuits.

And Jerome, who had a lizard expert's gullibility, was amused and titillated to be in the company of a former film star. Blandina would have loved to meet Pam. His ex-wife was overly fond of celebrities. But he brushed that thought aside. The memory of her thefts made his stomach clench.

How pleased Halla would be to see her old friend. Jerome often wondered if Halla felt lonely. It couldn't be easy being caught between worlds.

Pamela was utterly charming and interested in everything to do with Greenwater Park, particularly the lake. With pride, Jerome pulled out one of his father's aerial photographs and traced for her with his finger the lake's meandering path to the sea.

'These photos were taken from a helicopter years ago,' he explained, 'when my father was thinking of transporting his Bathysphere to the sea.'

'And did it work?' asked Pamela.

'Well, the channel was very narrow,' said Jerome. 'In the end, he used to get Milton to drive him to the coast. It was important to my father to be able to reach the sea easily, if need be. He was a little like my daughter. Loved all things wet! I used to think it was a phase with Louella. It drove my wife – I mean, my *ex*-wife – crazy. But I'm starting to think that Louella might have a watery future ahead of her!'

'How fascinating,' said Pamela. 'Then she must love the little sea-unicorn. I imagine sea-unicorns would be of interest to paying customers! Everyone loves a sea horse, after all. Humans are so predictable, aren't they?'

'Sea-unicorn?' said Jerome. 'Sea horses? Well, we haven't really investigated that possibility, you know, what with them being an endangered species. Saving the Water Creatures is all the rage these days, isn't it?'

Pamela frowned. 'Is it?'

'Oh, I keep hearing reports on the radio. What was it – mystery lipstick vigilantes or something. It's probably in the *Telegraph*, but we've been so busy with the park that I haven't read a newspaper in weeks! Quite nice, actually.'

'But what about Shirley?'

Jerome looked confused. 'Oh yes, well, she doesn't leave the folly very often. Those tail feathers make it hard for her to get around.'

'Tail feathers? How odd.'

'Is it?'

Their *tête-à-tête* was interrupted by Jerome's beeper, summoning him to the water slides. A small boy had fainted in the heat and required medical attention.

Jerome showed Pamela to the guest room on the ground floor. 'I've got extra wheelchairs,' he said, observing her awkward movements. 'I'll have Milton send one to your room. You look a little … well, tired.'

'Oh, it's just a bit of arthritis,' said Pamela. 'But that would be lovely.' She collapsed on the bed and gazed about the large room in raptures.

'The bathtub isn't fancy, but it's big,' said Jerome, pointing towards the en suite bathroom. 'And there's lots of lovely hot water! There's nothing a soak in a tub won't cure, especially after a long hot car journey. Keep those photos for a while if you're interested. Enjoy. I'll tell Thora and Halla that you're here. We'll meet up later for dinner! Now, if you'll excuse me …'

Jerome spun his wheelchair around and whizzed out of the room.

Pamela was parched. The long day had dried out her tail. She ran the bath and slipped in before it was filled. She immediately felt better.

With her arms held high so as not to dampen Jerome's photographs, Pamela studied the path to the sea.

It would be hard to leave this place right away. She felt as if she had come home.

## Chapter 50

Ever present in Jerome's thoughts was the fact that Thora and her mother had saved Snug from being turned into a croquet palace. Lately, with the money pouring in, he had been wondering how to thank his guests for all they had done. The arrival of their old friend Pamela gave him an idea. After attending to the small boy – who, it turned out, had mild heat stroke – he decided he would hold a surprise dinner party: his first in many years, and his debut as a newly minted bachelor.

He had an extensive network of contacts in the food world now and a number of favours he could call in. So that afternoon, he contacted some caterers in the area and hired a few assistants to help him organise a feast with an international flavour. There would be gefilte fish, gingko soup, fiddlehead ferns, kishke, deep-fried cods' tongues. Gravlax, sashimi and fried pickles. Tripe, blood sausage and marrow. And, of course, fresh-baked wholemeal bread cut into small squares and served alongside a deluxe ceramic pot of Patum Peperium.

✳

The heat of the day had resulted in another record-breaking attendance at the water park. Thora and Louella had worked non-stop since the gates opened at 9 a.m., and by closing time at 6 p.m. there was still a queue of sixteen people waiting to ride in the Bathysphere to the bottom of the lake. Two people could fit inside and each ride took eight minutes. It would be another hour and a half before they could pack up.

'You can't turn away a paying customer,' said Thora, taking a drink from her water bottle.

It was almost dark before they'd waved goodbye to the last stragglers, some of whom were disgruntled by the fact that they had not seen a mermaid. In fact, Halla had not been seen since lunchtime, a fact that made Thora a little anxious about Mr Walters.

But Jerome arrived and interrupted her worries with an extraordinary announcement.

'A special banquet is being served tonight in honour of one of your good friends, Thora. She's been waiting all afternoon at the house and is very keen to see you.'

Thora let out a delighted cry. 'It wouldn't be Shirley, would it?'

But Jerome was already wheeling away. 'It's very casual,' he called over his shoulder. 'Mr Walters can wear his cricket whites. No tails allowed! Except your mother's, of course. I demand she attend! I really mean it.'

Thora removed her windsurfing slippers and tipped the lake water out of them. Who could it be? They didn't have many friends – at least not in the Snug area. The tiny little hope flared in the back of her mind. *Could* it be Shirley?

'I loathe surprises,' said Louella.

'Oh, Louella,' chided Thora, 'sometimes I don't understand you at all! You will come to the dinner, won't you?

'Of course,' said Louella primly. 'It's not often that Daddy holds a dinner party.'

# chapter 51

When Thora arrived back at the folly to change, she discovered Mr Walters in the main room with a thick book, *An Organic Guide to English Gardens*, open on his lap.

Halla was sitting at the table reading aloud an article from the newspaper: *'Police estimate that close to seven hundred sea creatures from aquariums around England are unaccounted for ...'*

'Seven hundred and one, if we include dear little Shirley,' said Thora.

'Indeed,' said Mr Walters.

'It's all very mysterious,' said Halla, rather dreamily. 'Where is the fish-napper taking them all? And why? Louella says that the vigilante might be a marine biologist, because she seems to know what she's doing – taking only species that can survive in cold water.'

'You look as if there's something you want to say, Thora,' said Mr Walters.

'Yes,' said Thora formally. 'Jerome is holding an

impromptu bouquet. He would like everyone to attend. Mr Walters, you are to wear your cricket whites. Mother, you are the only tail allowed. In fact, he demands your presentation! There will be a special guest, as well. Someone who knows us. Perhaps it is Shirley.'

'Oh, I can't go,' said Halla.

'But Mother, why not?'

'I'm no good at dinner parties.'

Mr Walters stood up. 'Yes, Halla. You *will* go.'

Thora and Halla regarded Mr Walters with surprise. He rarely used such a stern tone of voice.

'Jerome has never once invited us to a formal dinner. He would not be doing it lightly. Out of respect, I think we all ought to attend.'

'Even Cosmo?' asked Thora.

'Most definitely,' said Mr Walters with a lopsided smile. 'Jerome might have difficulty remembering Cosmo's name, but he would miss him if he weren't there.'

Later, as he shaved in his capacious bedroom on the third floor, Mr Walters hoped he had not been too tough on Halla by demanding that she attend Jerome's dinner. He'd told her to go to the grotto to freshen up. He had sent Thora off to ask Milton to provide Halla with a wheelchair for the evening. She did not require a dress or skirt. They were amongst friends, and if the mystery guest was offended by Halla's tail, what sort of friend could this person be?

Mr Walters thought of the years that Halla had spent as an open-water swimming champion. The best in the world. But the deception had threatened to rob her of her shimmer. In time, her role as a mermaid exhibit here at Snug would also dull her phosphorescence. It had been a magical summer in some ways, and he was happy that they had managed to stop Jerome from turning Snug into a croquet palace. Halla had nursed him, and now that he was feeling a little better he could see that she herself was very pale. Her tail was an alarming milky purple, her hair a sickly greenish colour.

He was not exactly in tip-top shape himself. In the mirror, the face that looked back at him was that of an old man contemplating an English winter. Several months of flu had hollowed out his cheeks and etched a new series of boundary lines around his eyes.

Mr Walters could not *bear* the wet grey winter months. Not here. Not anywhere in England. And however wonderful it was to be involved, Greenwater Park was ultimately the Bidets' responsibility. Furthermore, it would have to close for the season. Louella would return to school, or at least be busy with her studies. Jerome had an enormous amount of work to do in the garden, preparing for the next year's harvest. And Jerome and Louella needed to spend time together, alone, as father and daughter. They were a family. Just as he was, with Thora and Halla.

As he had once been with his dear Imogen.

Once again he imagined her warming the teapot and having one of her little chats with him.

'Now, dear. Each journey begins with one step. I think you should consider Tasmania. Our honeymoon there was the trip of my life. Tasmania was the place I felt most at home in the world. Remember the time we got lost on Mount Wellington? Then we saw the sign for chook poo and we knew we would be all right.'

Mr Walters stared into the mirror and grinned.

Tasmania.

# Chapter 52

Thora wanted to do a cartwheel on the sloping wooden floor when she saw the feast spread out, smorgasbord-style, on the long table. The chandeliers were a little dusty, but the silver was polished and the linen sea-foam white. Snug House was starting to smarty up! She sat down next to Louella and spread her napkin on her lap. She didn't even feel like pretending that she was a princess at the Danish Royal Court. Or a guest of honour at a First Nations sweater lodge. She was happy to be Thora, with her good friends, in the main dining room at Snug. Cosmo sat at her feet waiting to be tossed a portion of gefilte fish, which he adored.

Jerome gestured towards the peacock. 'I think our guest will be very happy to see ... I am sorry, I can never for the life of me remember the beast's name! Is it Shirley?'

Thora gave him a puzzled look. 'Shirley? No, his name is Cosmo!'

'For the fifty-second time,' said Louella, exasperated.

The stairs creaked and Mr Walters entered the room, smelling of aloe-vera shaving foam and spray starch. Thora loved the way her Guardian Angle always managed to keep the creases of his cricket whites in the right places!

A few minutes later, Milton wheeled in Halla. 'You look lovely, Mother,' cried Thora happily.

'Over here,' directed Jerome, indicating the place at the head of the table. 'There should be plenty of tail space for you.'

Halla smiled. She gave no sign of wishing to be elsewhere. Her hair formed a golden wreath around her pretty ivory face. She must have scrubbed her tail, thought Thora, for it looked brighter than it had an hour ago.

Louella eyed the table warily. 'Where's the Marmite?'

'And now for … our guest of honour,' said Jerome.

Everyone turned to watch the third wheelchair roll into the dining room. Thora leaped up. 'Pamela!' They all stared. Mr Walters' blue eyes popped. Halla hugged herself. Cosmo stopped chewing his gefilte fish. Thora dashed around the table and embraced the unexpected guest. 'Pamela!

How *are* you? What have you been doing? How did you get here? I didn't know you knew the Bidets! I love your gold eyeshadow. And fake tan. Very gladiator!'

'There's nothing nicer than when old family friends meet up again. I do love a reunion,' said Jerome.

'Oh, Pamela is not my mother's friend,' said Thora.

Jerome swivelled in his wheelchair. 'Pardon?'

'In fact, they haven't even *met*. Until now, of course. I did try to arrange a species reunion, back on the *Loki*. Didn't I, Pamela? Mr Walters, you remember Pamela, of course.'

Mr Walters coughed. 'Yes, yes.'

Avoiding his eye, Pamela surveyed the table. 'What a stunning meal!'

Mr Walters wiped his brow. 'Yes, some of my favourite dishes!' He threw Halla a worried glance.

But Halla's mind was elsewhere. She was remembering the day when Thora returned from her first meeting with Pamela in the Thames. Thora had been so excited to meet another mermaid. But Halla had been preoccupied with Mr Walters' illness. She had not taken in the full meaning of 'another mermaid'. Her own species! Now that the two of them were sitting opposite one another, a question that had preoccupied Halla for the last ten years, and which she had always done her utmost to bat away, advanced towards her over the gravlax. Could Pamela know something about Thor?

'Mother?' said Thora. 'What's wrong?'

'I do love the … the tablecloth,' said Halla lamely. 'Is it Irish?'

'As a matter of fact, it is,' replied Jerome. 'A wedding gift. Not mine, but my parents'. I can't *tell* you how many meals it's seen. If we brighten the lights, we could probably read the spills like a map!'

'Oh, you are droll!' said Pamela.

'And have you seen your good friend Cosmo?' Jerome asked Pamela. He smiled, pleased to have remembered Cosmo's name.

'Cosmo?' said Pamela. 'Where have I heard that name before?'

Cosmo grabbed his scrap in his beak and crawled under the table, out of sight. Halla and Mr Walters exchanged glances. Jerome laughed uncertainly. His surprise party wasn't developing in the way he had anticipated. He couldn't put his finger on why, but for some reason he was reminded of another scene from *Neptune's Stepsister* when Pamela, playing the part of a famished mermaid, had pinched Neptune's trident to spear some flounder. She had been rather *too* convincing. He clapped his hands. 'Now, what can I pour everybody?'

Pamela was charming. But not charming enough to entrance Louella, who yawned over her second bowl of trifle and then announced that she was heading upstairs to bed.

Halla was fading too. Her tumult of emotions had had to be wrestled into silence. It was clear that Pamela was hiding her mermaidness from Jerome and that Halla's questions would have revealed Pamela's identity. No matter how urgently Halla wanted to speak – about her precious Thor, about the Sea Shrew, about the World Below – she could never tell tales about another mermaid. No one knew more painfully than Halla what it was like to live undercover. As a result, the numbingly polite chit-chat had drained her. Her tail was dry. She needed to return to the grotto.

Concerned about Halla, Mr Walters announced that he would wheel her across the lawn before he retired upstairs. 'I haven't eaten such delicious blood sausage in years. And the fiddleheads were perfection. So much tastier than sea kelp.'

'Hear, hear,' agreed Halla feebly.

'An inspired spread, Jerome,' added Mr Walters. 'A hymn to good food and witty conversation. Now, if you will forgive us ...'

'Goodnight, Halla! Goodnight, Mr Walters!' said Jerome. 'We should have gathered like this earlier. But it's been such a busy time! We'll do it again soon.'

Jerome, too, looked tired. 'Well, I'll leave you two old mates to catch up,' he said to Thora and Pamela. 'I've got to go and see if the food deliveries have arrived for tomorrow. You know where everything is? Goodnight, then. See you in the morning!'

'People in the country are so much more considerate than they are in the cities,' said Pamela, watching Jerome glide out of the room. 'I think I'm really quite a rural mermaid at heart.'

Thora pushed back her chair and groaned contentedly. 'I am so full. I've eaten more than an African elephant. Did you know that they grow to be over four metres tall?'

'No, I didn't,' said Pamela, turning her wheelchair so

she faced Thora directly. The sardine inflection in her voice was pronounced. She looked almost feverish. 'Now tell me all your news! I want to hear everything that's happened since we last met!'

Thora scrambled to fill her in on events.

'Well, we never discovered who stole the *Loki*. But she'll be ready for us to collect at the end of September. Maybe earlier. They have had to rebuild the entire hull because the damage was so extensive. And do you remember dear little Shirley?'

'Vaguely,' said Pamela carefully.

'Not a word.'

'What do you mean?'

'Didn't you know? She's been missing in action since the theft.'

'But Jerome said she was here,' said Pamela.

'He did?'

'Yes. When I first arrived.'

'He must have been talking about Cosmo,' said Thora with a sad laugh. 'No, we haven't seen Shirley since the *Loki* was stolen. She just disappeared into thin water. Which is an epical tragedy, because ...' Thora broke off and looked away for a moment, studying the flickering candle. 'Because she's rare and, according to Mr Walters, quite valuable. You never know what sort of scurvy old pirate might capture her and hold her to ransom. Mr Walters says that sea-unicorns are as rare as a squonk in a swamp.'

Pamela put down the ladyfinger she was nibbling and took a big gulp of water. 'I haven't heard from Miss Fishlock either.'

'Who is that?' asked Thora.

Pamela cursed herself. She'd completely forgotten that Thora had never met her former assistant. Well, no need to tell her now. It would only complicate things. 'Oh, nobody.'

'I bet she wouldn't like being described as nobody,' said Thora, deciding after all to help herself to another spoonful of trifle.

'Better that than some of the other words I could use to describe her.' Pamela's manner had turned brittle.

'And you heard nothing about the *Loki* after we left? I'm sorry we didn't visit you to tell you we were leaving London, but there wasn't a minute to waste. Mr Walters was worried that the officials would start to sniff around and try to haul Mother off to an aquarium and that sort of malarkey. And once we were here, we were flung right into the midst of the Croquet Wars. Then the idea came up for Greenwater Park and we've been busier than octopi on a construction site ever since.'

Since Thora's revelation that Shirley was missing, Pamela's mind had been reeling. Her eyes had taken on a black gloss and her cheeks flamed.

Suddenly her eyes lit on the ring around Thora's neck and clung to it – like someone who is drowning clings to a life ring thrown to them. 'I *did* enjoy the film you showed me in the *Loki*,' she said to Thora.

'The projectionist's ring is the last link to my earthly history,' replied Thora.

'I'm pleased to hear it's still working,' said Pamela.

'Like a Swiss cheese watch,' said Thora.

Pamela seemed to reach a decision. 'Unlike you, an old mermaid like me requires her bath and beauty sleep,' she said. 'I'd better take my tail off to the tub.'

'Let me help you.'

As Thora wheeled Pamela into her room a silver object fell to the floor.

'Oops-a-tulip, you dropped something.' She bent down and picked it up. 'What are these?'

'Just something to keep my nails looking nice.'

'They look like they could do some serious damage!'

Pamela took the nail clippers and, with her free hand, ran her fingers through her red mane. 'Thank you, Thora,' she said emotionally.

Thora looked surprised. 'For what?'

'For all you've done for me.'

'I haven't done anything!'

'You're a bit of a gimlet, but a good girl. Give an old lady a hug. I'm sorry. I feel quite teary.'

'No need to cry!' said Thora, leaning over to embrace Pamela. There was a funny clicking sound as they hugged. 'You just need a long soak in the tub and a good night's sleep. And tomorrow, you can come down and meet my mother properly. And maybe join her in the lake for a swim. Snug Lake is terrific fun! Goodnight! Don't let the jellyfish bite!'

# chapter 53

It was a soft, windlessly warm night, but as Thora made her way down the steps of the great old house to return to the folly, she felt strangely chilled, as if she'd finished a swim and forgotten to dry off.

Shivering, she looked up at the dark, star-speckled sky. The moon seemed to have scrubbed the stars with a particularly bright light. Her eyes sought out Sirius, her favourite constellation, then tracked a falling star to the black line of trees on the distant hills. A pulse of green in the blackness made her wonder if the star had exploded in the tree tops. The green pulsed again, like a well-lit heartbeat. In the darkness it suggested an emerald firefly. Then came the dull sound of tyres on gravel.

'What's going on out here?' It was Louella in her dressing gown, holding a torch in her hand. 'I was just falling asleep when I heard the car. Who could it be?'

'Maybe some aquanut wanting a midnight ride in the Bathysphere!' said Thora.

The driver ignored the DO NOT ENTER signs. When it looked as if the car was not going to stop at all, Louella flashed her torch at the driver and ran in front of the headlights.

There was the squeal of brakes and tearing of gravel as the pink station wagon skidded to a halt. It was the kind of car you'd expect to see Barbie drive out of Hamleys toy store on Oxford Street.

The driver sat very still then turned her head towards Thora.

The desperado with the creased face. White husky-dog eyes.

As it dawned on her where she'd seen those eyes before, green spangles drew her attention to the back of the car.

It was a green not found anywhere else on earth.

Thora pressed her face against the glass. '*Shirley!*' she shrieked.

# Chapter 54

The sparkles that surged through the aquarium were rainbow-coloured – tiny little beads of red, orange, yellow, blue, green and violet light.

Thora opened the door and unhooked the latch on top of the tank.

'Wait one minute. You stop that!' shouted the desperado.

Shirley swam into Thora's hand and wrapped her tail around her wrist. Thora drew her arm out of the aquarium.

The driver leaped from the car. 'Don't touch her!'

No one listened.

Louella watched, transfixed. 'Thora, what an adorable little creature!'

Thora held Shirley up against her cheek.

'Thora?' asked Miss Fishlock.

'That would be me,' replied Thora, saluting with her free hand. She took a few exultant steps and twirled on the tiptoe of her windsurfing slipper, lifting Shirley aloft like a star.

Louella laughed delightedly. 'You'll make her motion sick. She's so happy to see you!'

Miss Fishlock started after Thora, but Louella put out her hand to stop her. 'Let them be alone for a few minutes.'

Shirley was thinner and somehow looked older, more mature. But she pulsed with the familiar radiant green light. Thora walked towards the mulberry tree and sat underneath it on the grass.

'We have been very worried about you, Shirley. But Mr Walters said that you would survive. And he was right. You are an empress! So much has happened, I don't know where to begin.'

Shirley gazed into Thora's eyes. For a while, there on the lawn, the half-mermaid and the green sea-unicorn basked in the warmth of each other's company, oblivious to everything and everyone around them.

'We must never be parted again,' said Thora. 'Families are supposed to stay together.'

Thora and Shirley joined the others next to the front steps.

'Come here, Thora,' Louella finally called. 'Miss Fishlock has a very interesting tale to tell!'

Miss Fishlock started off calmly but then broke down and wept. As she dried her glasses, she repeated the story she'd just told Louella.

They had started out searching for Thora, she explained between sobs, but had been sidelined by their mission to release the sea creatures.

And that was what they thought they were doing when they'd pulled up at Snug. A message had come in on the ham radio a few hours earlier, saying that there was a large sea creature being held in captivity at Greenwater Park. They'd arrived late at night, to avoid detection.

Before Thora could respond, Miss Fishlock went on to admit to her role in the theft and the sinking of the *Loki*. She did not mention any other names or make excuses for herself. Nor did she expect Thora to forgive her. 'I understand entirely if you would like me to leave.'

Miss Fishlock might have the gruffness of an old desert cowboy, but it was clear from the way she regarded Shirley that she loved the little green sea-unicorn with all her heart.

Thora accepted her apologies with a vigorous handshake. 'It's a sad tragical odyssey we've been on in some ways, but if the *Loki* hadn't sunk, I might never have got to know my great friend Louella as well as I have.'

224

Louella straightened her spectacles and smiled.

'And Greenwater Park might never have been built.'

'Nor would all those sea creatures have been saved,' said Louella. 'I noticed the story in Mr Walters' newspaper a few weeks ago. Halla and I have been following it.'

'Really?' said Miss Fishlock.

'Yes, for it raises interesting issues about conservation that I would like to study in greater depth.' Louella stopped herself before she began to lecture. 'I've been thinking that the people behind it must be very noble. And brave.'

Shirley looked away modestly.

'What did you do before you became a vigilante?' Louella asked Miss Fishlock.

'I worked for a washed-up film actress who made her money selling tropical fish to collectors and aquariums.'

'I see,' said Louella. 'And where is she now? Behind bars, I hope!'

'I don't know,' said Miss Fishlock, her eyes darkening.

In the dining room, the dishes from the feast had not yet been cleared away. Thora wiped some glasses with a napkin and poured three glasses of tonic water, which she spiced up with a dash of pepper and a squeeze of mango. She was still shivering. She hoped she had not caught Mr Walters' flu. She found an old cut-glass port decanter for Shirley and filled it with sea water from the back of the station wagon.

Miss Fishlock leaned across the table and helped herself to a perogy. Thora rested her chin on her arms and watched Shirley twirl in her decanter, releasing grey rings remarkably like Cherokee smoke signals.

'Looks like Shirley is trying to tell us something,' said Miss Fishlock, dabbing her mouth with a napkin.

'You're right,' said Thora. 'What is it, Shirley?'

Looking distressed, Shirley pointed with her snout and horn at Thora's chest.

'What?' laughed Thora, looking down.

The smile died on her lips. The projectionist's ring was gone!

# Chapter 55

'No wonder I felt all shivery and strange!' Thora said faintly, searching the pockets of her wetsuit. Not once since her grandmother had given her the ring had she not known its whereabouts. It was as much a part of her as her scales, her blowhole, her purple shins!

It was also her only link to her father.

Her mind flowed rapidly backwards through the evening to the arrival of Miss Fishlock and Shirley. Then it reversed up the stairs and along the hallway to Pamela's room, the kiss, the toenail clippers. 'Pamela!'

She jumped up and dashed out of the room.

'Pamela?' said Miss Fishlock.

Louella nodded. 'Pamela P. Poutine. The French Canadian dish.'

In her decanter, Shirley twisted like a snake and black sparkles fizzed in the water. Her eyes blazed.

'What's wrong with her?' asked Louella, alarmed.

'It's the mention of THAT NAME,' said Miss Fishlock. 'I try *never* to say it. Shirley goes wild when I do!'

'But why? She's just a tarty old bore who wears too much make-up.' Louella snorted. 'Comes here saying she's a famous actress!'

'Here?' said Miss Fishlock.

Louella stood up. 'Daddy is so gullible. It really drives me mad sometimes. But what does Pamela have to do with the ring?'

'Did I hear you correctly?' said Miss Fishlock. 'Did you say that Pamela P. Poutine's *here*?'

'Yes,' said Louella. 'Since this afternoon. Too long, in other words!'

Thora returned, pulling on her ponytail. 'Pamela's gone,' she said flatly.

'She's here, she's gone – which is it?' demanded Miss Fishlock.

'How can she be gone?' questioned Louella. 'I mean, what on earth is going on?'

'What in *sea*, you mean,' said Thora. 'I searched her room. Everywhere. *She's nowhere!*'

'I'll be right back,' said Louella. 'I want to check whether Milton's seen her.'

As Louella raced off, a few details splintered Thora's mind: Pamela's early interest in the ring; her offer to buy it; her flushed face as she examined it. And, upon reflection, it was very odd how Pamela had arrived at Snug out of the blue, claiming to be good friends with everybody.

'I ... know ... what's ... happened. She came here,'

said Miss Fishlock, 'to steal Shirley.'

'What!' cried Thora.

Miss Fishlock frowned, concentrating. She looked at her toes. 'The last time I spoke to Pamela was on the ham radio from the *Loki*. I told her I was about to crash into the bridge. I thought she'd told me, you see, to steal the tug.'

'But the *Loki* is not a tug,' said Thora indignantly.

'Yes,' Miss Fishlock waved her hand impatiently, 'I know. But I didn't know that when I stole it. I thought Pamela wanted the entire boat. She didn't. I made a blunder. She wanted the *jug*.'

Thora looked at her blankly.

'Shirley was in the jug at the time. Pamela wanted the jug. Don't you see?'

'Pamela wanted Shirley?' said Thora. 'But Shirley was with *you*.'

'Yes, but Pamela thought that she was with *you*!' said Miss Fishlock. 'And she came here to Snug to get her.'

'But Shirley *wasn't* here … So she stole the ring instead,' said Thora.

The words hung in the space between them. Once spoken, Thora knew, beyond a doubt, that they were true.

'Oh, Shirley, I didn't listen to you. All of this could have been avoided if I had paid attention to you that first time we met Pamela in the Thames. You *knew* what she was doing.'

Shirley looked down. A swirl of red lights appeared. They formed an exclamation mark.

Louella reappeared. Breathlessly, she told them that Milton had seen someone in the lake when he was returning from night fishing; but when he'd called to her, she'd dived underwater. Then he'd found a mound of clothes by the edge of the lake. A tomato-coloured skirt, a white blouse and a straw hat.

Louella rolled up the sleeves of her dressing gown. 'You've got to go after Pamela – this minute.'

'Yes,' said Thora. 'But I want you to come in the Bathysphere!'

'But Thora, the Bathysphere travels at five kilometres an hour. And you can swim as fast as a dolphin – for forty minutes!'

'But I'd like you to be there. In case something goes wrong.'

'Nothing will go wrong, Thora. Leave. Go on!'

Thora's lower lip trembled. 'But I'm afraid.' She crossed her arms and hunched her shoulders. Her voice came out as a whisper. 'I've never been very deep.'

# chapter 56

The aerial photographs made Pamela's escape route clear.

The lake connected to the stream.

The stream connected to the river.

The river connected to the waterfall.

The waterfall connected to the canal.

The canal connected to the sea.

Pamela was no open-water swimmer. She had been afraid to return to her element, her departure had enraged the Sea Shrew and led to her banishment. But now she was streaking towards the sea, faster than she'd ever swum before.

To date, Pamela's entire life seemed composed of such moments – of escapes, deceptions, lies. But there was a purity to this journey, perhaps because if successful it would signal a sea change.

She swam and swam, across the lake, up the stream, along the river and down the waterfall. She swam as if in a dream towards the open water. Towards freedom. Towards Dublin, where she would call Mr Oto and arrange a meeting in Tokyo. Mr Oto had paid forty million dollars for a share in a Hollywood studio. He'd practically *started* Kabukiwood. What would he pay for a ring with such magical cinematic powers? Compared with the ring, Shirley seemed as valuable as a piece of shrimp brine.

Pamela calculated that it would take her a week or two to make the journey to Tokyo.

# chapter 57

Louella, Thora, Miss Fishlock and Milton heaved the Bathysphere from the pier into Milton's waiting speedboat.

Shirley watched from the lake as they packed the boat with the oxygen cable, two cylinders, and the rope that Thora would tug on when she spied Pamela.

While Milton checked the stuffing box at the top of the Bathysphere (they did not want any leaks), Louella slipped behind a tree to change into her wetsuit and Thora sprinted over to the grotto to let her mother in on events. But she wasn't there.

Thora found her in the folly, gathering together their few possessions. Halla calmly received the news of what Thora planned to do, though it alarmed and disappointed her to learn the truth about Pamela's character. There would be no leisurely discussions with the other mermaid about Halla's missing husband, Thora's father; about the Sea Shrew; about watery childhoods and rebellious adolescent longings for the World Above. Not now, anyway.

Halla put her arms around her daughter and kissed her cheek. 'You be very, very careful,' she said. 'You haven't spent a lot of time in the deep. Anything could happen.' Though a part of her wanted to, she didn't try to stop Thora. The projectionist's ring meant everything. To both of them.

'I'll tell Jerome you've taken the Bathysphere,' she added. 'I need to speak to him anyway.'

Thora looked around. 'What's this, Mother? Are you packing?'

'I think, darling, that our time at Snug is drawing to an end.'

＊

Before she joined the others on the boat, Thora had one more thing to do. She scribbled a note. 'Cosmo, could you do me a favour? Deliver this to Mr Walters. He's on the third floor. You'll know the room – he always sleeps with the window open.'

```
Dear Guardian Angle,

    We  have  gone  on  a  quest  to  recapture  the
projectionist's  ring  from  Pamela  P.  Poutine.  We
believe  she  stole  it  and  is  heading  for  the  open
sea,  where  she  plans  to  sell  it  to · a  wicked
collector. Will explain everything later.

    Love, Thora.
```

## chapter 58

It had been many years since Milton's sea-captain days, and in that time, outboard engines had changed quite a lot. As he opened the throttle he almost lost the Bathysphere.

'You nitwit,' yelled Miss Fishlock, grabbing the steering wheel. 'Let *me*!'

Thora and Louella hung on in the back, their faces misted by the steady spray of water. Shirley had never looked greener. She perched on the edge of the extra life jacket, her tail and belly resting on the wet floor. The boat surged across the lake, slowing slightly at the entrance to the stream.

'There you go, dear,' said Miss Fishlock, stepping aside so Milton could resume the wheel. When he glanced back at Thora and Louella, his face was tinged yellow. 'Pass me the ginger tablets,' he said wanly.

'No time to be ill,' ordered Louella.

'I'm trying not to be!' shouted Milton, popping a lozenge under his tongue.

'From the Bristol Channel, she'll be heading up to the Irish Sea,' said Miss Fishlock.

When they reached the river Milton accelerated until they came to a shallow creek.

'Stop!' shouted Thora. She leaned over the side of the boat and plucked a silver and red speckled hoop from a tangle of weeds.

'Pamela's earring!' exclaimed Louella.

'Not far to the sea now,' said Milton, pointing ahead to a small waterfall. 'Just the canal to go after this.'

'But how do we get over the waterfall?' asked Louella.

'Hold on!' shouted Milton, as the boat tumbled over.

'It's like white-river rafting in Jasper National Park,' cried Thora. 'Lean forward!'

Milton popped another ginger lozenge in his mouth and mopped his brow. They'd made it. The sea was a few miles straight ahead.

Before Thora could concentrate on the task ahead, she had something to tell her friend. 'Louella, do you know we have to go soon?'

'The sooner the better,' said Louella, eyeing the Bathysphere hungrily.

'I mean, once we get the ring back – even if we *don't* – we have to leave Snug.'

Louella looked stricken. 'But you just got here! What about the water park? Snug without a mermaid? Impossible!'

'Now, you two,' interrupted Miss Fishlock, 'listen up! It's time to review our strategy.'

Thora attached one end of the rope to the Bathysphere. 'I'll dive in, holding this. We've got forty minutes.'

'And I'll get into the Bathysphere and wait for the signal,' said Louella, looking down.

'When I see Pamela,' said Thora, 'I'll pull on the rope three times.'

'Then Milton will lower me after you.'

'And I'll keep the Bathysphere pumped with oxygen,' said Miss Fishlock.

'Minor detail,' said Louella, her excitement muted by Thora's news.

# Chapter 59

It was a lifetime since Pamela had left the security of the Thames. She'd forgotten the wild beauty of the ocean floor.

There were sturgeon, cuttlefish, wall-eyed cod. There were silvery clouds of flickering anchovies and cuckoo wrasse. There were starfish, sponges, jellyfish and carp. But what stirred her emotions and made her feel overwhelmed with homesickness was the colour. After the relentless, grinding grey of London, the deep sea was pulsing with blue, green and yellow bioluminescent lights. They reminded Pamela of the colour of her tail when she had first gone ashore in the World Above. Now she remembered the coral trees of her childhood, flecked orange, green, white and pink; the black bar soldierfish, sharpnose puffers and flamingo tongue snails. How, when she returned home from school, she would pause to greet the basket starfish that lazed under the current, their arms open wide to the undulating water.

How far she had travelled away from her ambition!
How low she had sunk.

If the sea life all around her knew of her betrayal,
they weren't letting on. They greeted her. They
smiled. They flitted along beside her. How liberating
it was to glide through the water! To be free of
cumbersome walking sticks, rustling skirts, ham radios,
station wagons. To be naked in the weightless indigo
sea where, like a great southern right whale, she could
twist and turn in an effortless dance. A place where her
tail was at home. Where her whole being belonged – if
only the Sea Shrew would forgive and forget!

Surrounded by her own kind, Pamela felt a sudden
stab of sorrow about what she had become, and a
yearning to recapture her younger, truer self – the
starry-eyed mermaid with a dream.

Ahead, she saw a gathering of flickering fish behind
a wall of coral. The luminescent light poured through
a small gap in the wall and lit the cliff face opposite.

She had an idea.

# Chapter 60

Despite her scuba-diving lessons, Louella had not been deeper than six metres – the depth of Snug Lake. The prospect of descending to the ocean bed made her head reel.

This took her by surprise for she was not the sort of person who experienced stage fright. She had stood before dozens of people more learned than she, more experienced, more insightful, and talked about the mysteries of the sea. Now, as she prepared to descend in the Bathysphere for the first time in open water, she felt that everything until this moment had been mere preparation.

She felt, suddenly, that she knew nothing.

Nevertheless, her heroes urged her on. In addition to Thora's face she saw the faces of Beebe and Barton, Sylvia Earle, Jacques Cousteau, Don Walsh, Jacques Piccard.

Everyone she had ever heard or read about, everyone she had learned from and loved was right

there. With her. Encouraging her on.

Her grandfather. Her mother. Her father.

Even the good bits of Blandina.

'Are you going to be OK?' asked Thora.

'Brilliant,' said Louella, with a smile.

'Go,' ordered Miss Fishlock.

Louella waved as Thora jumped into the water. 'Couldn't be better.'

'OK, Shirley. Take us to her.' It was cold and blue and silent under the water. Thora's words came out in a rush of bubbles that made Shirley smile.

Shirley pointed her horn in a northerly direction and swam using all of her sea-horsepower and her rather well-developed sonar-tracking skills, propelled by her wings. In her wake streamed a thin but sure trail of yellow lights.

She guessed that Pamela would be swimming deep, to avoid detection by staying in the darker water, and that she would be travelling at approximately the rate of a bluefin tuna.

Shirley had not been in the open sea since her flight from the mangrove forest in Bohol. Back then, its immensity had overwhelmed her, especially the swells in the South China Sea. The changes in the light had also caused her alarm. First the golden light of land. Then the green of the sea. Then, deeper, the intense blue.

But she was older now, had been through a hedge or two, as Mr Walters would say, and knew the ropes. Thora was at her side. She had a mission. She was not afraid.

Shirley and Thora had been swimming along the sandy sea bed for a good twenty-five minutes when they noticed a strong white light about a kilometre away. It was not the usual sort of phosphorescence you came across on the ocean floor. It was static. It resembled the light given off by the fluorescent lights in the London Aquarium.

Thora almost laughed when it dawned on her.

She gave three yanks on the rope, to tell Louella to begin her descent.

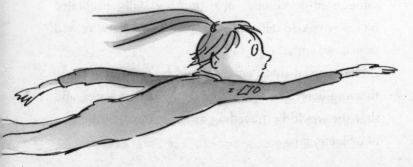

# chapter 61

Shirley and Thora arrived at the site of the strange static light. It was very bright.

They stared with awe at the underwater spectacle before them. They were so amazed they barely looked up when Louella dropped into sight in the Bathysphere.

An old film called *Dance Me a Mermaid* was playing (the only print of which had disappeared with the sinking of the SS *Messiah* II in 1959), starring Esther Williams and now … Pamela P. Poutine!

The bright light from the projector shone on Pamela's face. She was dancing masterfully alongside the great swimming champion and film star, and her dreamy, shimmery presence suggested that it was she and not Esther Williams who was the real star of the film.

It was beautiful to watch. The film's colours were intense, as if pigmented by a phosphorescent rainbow, so bright they almost hurt the eyes.

And the performance was moving. Poignant.

Pamela was by no means a young mermaid. Her tail was well padded. Her hair an unnatural shade of red. Her arms a bit wobbly. But she danced with grace and passion, her tail flicking the ghostly waterweeds, her arms forming bracelets around the darting fish.

Whatever apprehension she had about meeting the Sea Shrew was momentarily cast aside.

The scales had fallen from her spirit. She looked young and happy. Her face was shining.

Louella advanced towards the coral wall where the miracle was taking place and studied it closely.

Pamela had inserted the ring she had stolen into a small hole in the coral reef. Huddling on the other side, a school of helpful fish acted as substitutes for a projector, fuelling the ring with the light necessary to throw up an image on the cliff face opposite. Their glow heightened the film's colours in a way Thora and Louella had never seen before.

There was no scientific explanation. But this fact did not trouble Louella as it once might have done. On her descent she had observed herring, bright yellow sea sponges, marine turtles and sea scorpions. She was so enthralled that she almost forgot the sadness that had flooded her on hearing Thora's announcement about leaving Snug. She almost forgot the reason she was down here in the first place! Quite simply, she was having the time of her life.

Louella Bidet – AQUANAUT. How different the

animals were in their natural habitat, how particular and interesting their personalities!

I will never eat fish again, she promised herself, staring at Pamela's vibrant fishy tail through the peephole.

# chapter 62

Without warning, a curtain of darkness fell.

All the dazzling colours fled.

Pamela opened her eyes. Her face was cold and fearful. She could see a strange silhouette coming towards her. In fact, there were hundreds of small, rather familiar-looking creatures advancing in her direction. Was it the Sea Shrew with her minions? But no, it was a young voice that spoke.

'This ring is mine,' it said. 'And I'm taking it back.'

Pamela was a mermaid torn from a dream.

'I want you to apologise to Shirley for trying to steal her,' said Thora.

Pamela looked like a ghost crab on a fishmonger's slab.

Thora, Shirley and Louella now formed an accusing circle around Pamela P. Poutine – along with all the fish that had been bossed into donating their bioluminescence to power Pamela's underwater fantasy, a good number of the sea critters Pamela had held captive in the Saltworks Luxury Flats, plus some of the faster-swimming creatures from the tanks that Miss Fishlock and Shirley had liberated.

Spiroworms, blennes and six dogfish joined them. An albino sea-horse. Two little angler fish. A goatfish. A parrot fish. A slipper lobster. Word travels fast underwater. Some just wanted to see what was going on. Others wanted revenge.

Soon the crowd was quite large.

'You're going to take me to the Sea Shrew,' Pamela said, in the saddest voice Thora had ever heard.

'No,' said Thora.

'Kill me?'

'No.'

'Sell me to Mr Oto?' Pamela began to weep. 'Please don't sell me to Mr Oto.'

'Who is Mr Oto?' said Thora.

'You've got the ring. What more do you want?'

There was silence.

Finally a faint glimmer of understanding registered in Pamela's black eyes.

'I see. You want me to apologise. OK. I'm sorry, Shirley. I'm sorry, Thora. I'm sorry to all of you out there I captured. I'm sorry, too, to all of your cousins and uncles and stepsisters — to everyone and everything I have hunted down to sell on the black market.'

'Not very heartfelt,' said Thora. 'If you were

auditioning for a part, I don't think I'd be able to give it to you.'

'I've betrayed you all!' cried Pamela, crumpling.

'Yes,' said Thora encouragingly. 'I think you're getting the idea.'

'Then I can go?' said Pamela, rubbing her hands together.

Thora shook her head. Shirley shook her head. In the Bathysphere, Louella, too, shook her head.

Afterwards, none of them would be able to agree who had the idea first.

'But what do you all *want* from me?'

'We want what *you* want.'

'Whatever do you mean by that?'

Thora swam over to Pamela. They were so close, their noses touched.

'We want your shimmer!'

                                                Grotto Palace

                                                  Snug Lake

                                                      Snug

                                                Snugshire, UK

Dear Mr Oto,

I am writing to terminate the contract you already
terminated, due to the fact that I will no longer
be available to help you or your clients.

   I have recently been selected to feature in an
ongoing role as principal mermaid at Snug Lake. It
is a role that celebrates my natural attributes
without unduly exploiting them - and therefore
releases me into an honest life. I have good reason
to believe the job is mine forever, which will make
it the longest-running show in the history of
humankind. Even longer than *The Mousetrap*.

                                                Yours truly,

                                                Pamela P. Poutine.

cc. Lee.

Dearest Your Deepness,

How are you, my great and worthy aquanaut? I hope this finds you haler and heartier than a Tasmanian abalone diver!

I want to report first that Shirley is *abundantly thrilled* with the mangrove forest that you and your father planted in the lower hull. Also, as you predicted, the sea-unicorn flap that you invented allows her to come and go with ease, granting her total freedom to explore the sea when and if she wants. Sometimes she goes off for a few days. Sometimes she takes swims with Mother. But always she comes home.

Although we loved our time at Snug, it is a relief to be back in *our* home. I am sure that the new paint job will soon be peeling off the hull like strips of manna gum. But as I told you, the *Loki* is a peely sort of boat and not even an overhaul can change her true nature.

I shall always treasure the logbook you gave me (with the fold-out science graph paper and built-in calculator), but I cannot promise that I will use it only for field notes. Already I have written in it a poem, which I shall transcript for you at a later date. For now, I suspect, you want only the facts rather than subjunctive musings.

We all greatly enjoyed our farewell tea party on the lawn. Please don't feel bad for crying as you waved us a-dew! The only reason I too did not weep squonk-sized tears is because of my mermaid origins, for, as you know, mermaids don't cry. Their tails just grow pale. And indeed, my ankles and feet blanched to a ghostly shade at our parting and remained pallid for many days. Even now, as I look down, I see only the faintest tincture of purple rising up through my toes.

I am pleased that Miss Fishlock and Milton have become bosomy buddies. Everyone needs a friend, or, as Mr Walters would say, 'a warming drop of Scotch whisky in the blood'. Will they head to the Philippines right after the wedding? A honeymoon spent saving sea-horses sounds very noble and romantic to me.

On a culinary note, Mr Walters has just finished a Ritz cracker spread generously with Gentleman's Relish. I told him that it might be considered unethical to eat a spread composed of dead anchovies (you will be happy to hear that I have sworn off cod cheeks), but he says that he is now too old and too ugly to change his ways.

We are all still talking about Pamela, of course. I still remember my first meeting with her, and I will never forget the sardine infection of her voice, her ghost-crab hair or the interesting way she ambulated on land. She may not have a heart of gold, but I think there may be some bronze in it, for she showed herself at the end to have some winning ways.

Mother says there is a poetical symmetry to her fate. She promised that she was not cross when Jerome toasted Pamela as the most natural performing mermaid he had seen. And Mr Walters assures me that Pamela is perfectly designated for the job as mermaid-in-residence at a country estate. It lets her do what she always wanted and keeps her out of trouble. Forever! Mermaids live to be about 300 years old, so Pamela will be giving shows in Snug Lake to your very own grandchildren ... if you have them. I expect it won't be easy if you plan to spend a lot of time 11,000 metres down in your Bathysphere.

Talking of trouble, Mother is still fumigating over news she heard from Miss Fishlock on the ham radio. A journalist named Tinny Tennant is trying to raise a flusterbuss in the papers, saying that Halla tricked swimming officials by failing to declare her tail. Tinny is calling for Mother to return all her gold medals, but Mother sent them to an Indian charity long before we got to London.

We all (even Mr Walters) felt a little sad at the news that Pamela had revealed everything about herself in an in-depth interview with Tinny (which Mr Walters said was rather shallow). But I heard that the interview resulted in more record-breaking attendances at Greenwater Park!

Ever since it was decided that we would make Australia our next destination, Mr Walters has been *much* happier. He even bought a new portable iron and flat board at the market stall in Santa Lucia to press his brand-new cricket whites.

We are all most grateful for the bank account that your father set up in our name. Who would have thought that our summer wages at Snug Lake would give us a new release on life? We all assumptioned that we were sunk when the *Loki* went down.

To prepare for Australia we have traded our Marmite for Vegemite and are brushing up on Strine Stalk! It won't be long before I can speak a new language! Useful if I happen to bump into boogy-boarders in the Tasman Sea. I have heard that Hobart Town is a nice city with a view of a snow-capped mountain and a salamander market. Mr Walters would like to take us to places he went to with his wife on their honeymoon - though no fish restaurants allowed!

Cosmo seems excited about our latest adventure too. He is, after all, from Flinders Island, which lies just at the top-tip of the state!

I hope that your new home-study plan with the school proves fortifying. I expect you'll be very busy with your part-time job with the National Geographic Teen Submersibles Programme. Perhaps you can arrange a bit of field study in Oz? I hear that the bioluminescence is spectacular in the Indian Ocean off Perth!

Mother sends you and your father her deepest phosphorescence.

I send you all of my rising shimmer.

Farewell!

Thora.

P.S. Write if you remember.

P.P.S. When you asked me in the tent that night if I'd ever kissed a boy, did you also mean *had a boy kissed me*? If not, the answer is no. If yes, then yes. His initials are R. R.

P.P.P.S. I probably don't have to tell you this is highly calcified information.

Photo © Dan Johnson

Gillian Johnson grew up in Winnipeg, where she spent her winters speed skating at Sargent Park Oval and her summers swimming in Lake Winnipeg. She now lives in England and Tasmania with her husband, writer Nicholas Shakespeare, and their two sons, Max and Benedict.

**More Thora from Hodder Children's Books:**

## THORA

*Gillian Johnson*

'Ten years at sea, ten years on land ...'

It's time for Thora – half-mermaid, half-human – to leave the sea and join the rest of us on dry land. She's ten now, and the Sea Shrew's prophecy says that her days in the deep are done.

Leaving her mermaid mother and taking her pet peacock, Cosmo, Thora does her best to settle down in the seaside town of Grimli. But trouble is brewing – as it so often is when Thora's around – and she comes face to face with Frooty de Mare, a fat-cat businessman who hates mermaids.

Thora's nothing if not determined, though. She'll stop Frooty's sinister plans, whether he likes it or not ...